Determined to put a hint of space between them even if she couldn't will herself to just walk away, Natalie flattened a hand to his chest.

The hard, muscled wall of his chest.

"I'm complimented you want to kiss me, but that's not included in the bed-and-breakfast package."

Max chuckled, the rumble of his laugh vibrating against her hand. "That's the nicest put-down I've ever received."

Gaining strength, she let out her own low laugh, eyebrows arching, taking him in, trying to focus on the crisp September air instead of his musky scent. Or the way the shadows played up his bad-boy mystique. "I imagine you don't get told no often."

"Another compliment. For someone who is rejecting me, you're doing it very nicely." His voice was still throaty, and he swallowed, eyes fixed on hers.

"So you hear me saying no to your advance?"

He nodded his head, the line of his lips growing taut. "I hear you. No is no. I just want you to remember I still feel the same way. I want to kiss you. Very much. And if you decide you want to act on this attraction, I'm not going anywhere anytime soon."

* * *

Taking Home the Tycoon
is part of the series Texas Cattleman's Club:
Blackmail—No secret—or heart—
is safe in Royal, Texas…

TAKING HOME THE TYCOON

BY
CATHERINE MANN

First Published in Great Britain 2017
By Mills & Boon, an imprint of HarperCollins*Publishers*
1 London Bridge Street, London, SE1 9GF

© 2017 Harlequin Books S.A.

Special thanks and acknowledgement are given to Catherine Mann
for her contribution to the Texas Cattleman's Club: Blackmail series.

ISBN: 978-0-263-06982-2

Printed and bound in Great Britain
by CPI Antony Rowe, Chippenham, Wiltshire

USA TODAY bestselling author **Catherine Mann** has won numerous awards for her novels, including both a prestigious RITA® Award and an *RT Book Reviews* Reviewers' Choice Award. After years of moving around the country bringing up four children, Catherine has settled in her home state of South Carolina, where she's active in animal rescue. For more information, visit her website, catherinemann.com.

To Vee, Sharon, Tiffany and all the volunteers
who make such an incredible difference
through the Sunshine State Animal Rescue.

One

For self-made cybersecurity billionaire Max St. Cloud, his life as a teen on the unforgiving streets of LA—panhandling, Dumpster diving for his next meal and hot-wiring cars for cash—seemed like a distant dream. Fifteen years later, hotshot Max enjoyed the hell out of his life in Seattle.

He adored his fleet of fast cars and hangar full of planes. His state-of-the-art modern marvel of a home was any techie's wet dream. He had his pick of women equally as committed to their professions. And he was married to St. Cloud Security Solutions, his corporate computer and building security firm.

So why in the hell was he sitting here in small-town Royal, Texas, sporting one helluva hard-on for a scrubbed, fresh-faced woman wearing mom jeans?

The ginger-haired beauty seated in the wingback beside him seemed unaware of his dilemma. A good or bad thing? He wasn't sure.

Digital tablet on his knee, he shifted in his leather chair, one of a pair by the fireplace in a meeting room at the Texas Cattleman's Club's lodge. Given he'd been called in as a security expert, he should be focused on this latest interview into a cyberwar being waged on the citizens of Royal.

Those were the key words: *should be*. He stole another glance at the woman beside him.

Clearing his throat, Max forced himself to take notes on his tablet because the odds of him remembering the details of this conversation with Natalie Valentine were next to nil. He stared at his notes about her: twenty-nine years old, war-widowed mother of two, wedding-dress designer, owner of the Cimarron Rose Bed and Breakfast in the center of town.

The simple facts didn't come close to revealing how damned appealing he found her.

"Mrs. Valentine—do you mind if I call you Natalie?"

"That's fine. Of course." She scratched a finger along the flour stain on her denim-covered thigh—her empty ring finger. "Actually, I prefer it."

The flash of pain in her eyes made him feel like an ass for jonesing over another guy's wife. Even a dead guy. Especially a dead guy. "I appreciate your taking time from your business day to speak with me."

"I'm still fairly new to the town. Surely there are people better suited than I am to share about the personalities in this area." Her fitted green T-shirt only made her massive emerald eyes glitter all the more. Her shoulder-length red hair was swept up into an unfussy ponytail. Little pretense. Raw beauty. And those eyes. Damn, they were intrinsically vulnerable and full of heart, yet the tip of her chin spoke of spirit just begging to be uncovered.

He recognized grit when he saw it, a kindred spirit. "I have a different take on you being too new to help. It's my experience that newcomers can also offer an objective perspective."

But the stakes were high on this security-consulting gig. Max had been called in by his longtime friend Chelsea Hunt—Chels—to help trace who was waging cybersmears on the good citizens of Royal. Chels had been one of his few true friends back in his early twenties. They'd both been hungry hackers with a bent for justice during a time she ran to LA to get away from her overprotective parents. But Chels had a more cultured upbringing. She'd helped him smooth out his rougher edges as he sought entry into the legitimate business world. She'd believed in him when no one else did. She'd been the sister he'd never had, cheering him on.

So some wannabe troll was hell-bent on destroying the lives of members of Royal's Texas Cattleman's Club? The sorry son of a bitch had picked the wrong firewalls to infiltrate. As far as Max was concerned, once a hacker, always a hacker. He was certain he could beat this amateur...or team. He had a hunch it wasn't one man or woman working alone...

"Mr. St. Cloud—"

"You're Natalie. I'm Max."

"Yes, then, um, Max, I'll try to help, but I'm usually running full tilt at my bed-and-breakfast." Natalie fidgeted with her simple silver watch, checking the time. "I don't mean to rush you, but I have dough rising for bread and pastries that I need to check on soon."

With each breath, her chest rose and fell faster, which happened to draw his eyes to the pink rose logo in an oval between her breasts. The paneled walls with trophies and historical artifacts closed in on him. The space seemed tighter. More intimate.

Mom jeans. A T-shirt. And the thought of tasting pastry filling on her lips.

Seriously?

"I realize your time is precious and I'll try to make this quick." Quick? Quickie… Damn, she sent his mind down distracting paths. So much for logical, techie objectivity. "You would be surprised at the details you hear without consciously registering them. And there are impressions gained in passing. You have the heartbeat of the town with your B and B…and with the wedding dresses you make."

Surprise turned her cheeks pink, her eyes widening and lips parting ever so slightly. "You know about my dresses?"

"I do my research," he said simply. "Experience with individuals in your line of business leads me to conclude that people talk to you, a lot. They share their life stories—about their children, their dates, their dogs, hell, even their medical history. They even, dare I say, gossip."

"I don't think of it as gossip really. I prefer to believe they feel comfortable at my B and B, whether they're spending the night or just stopping to join in a hot breakfast." Absently, she fingered her watchband.

"And there's no counselor-patient confidentiality involved in pastry making and stitchery."

She laughed, a full-throated, sexy laugh that relaxed stress lines from her pretty face. "Clearly."

"So I would like to pick your brain about…just impressions." He hated seeing the smile fade from her lips and her eyes, but he did have a job to accomplish. "I'm not asking you to implicate anyone. It's up to me to put together a whole picture that points to the culprit or gives ideas for ways to smoke him or her out. So if you're comfortable just talking…let me do my thing."

Her eyebrows shot up. "Do your thing? Is that computer-tech talk out West?"

Well, hell. So much for the badass-businessman persona he'd cultivated from his street-rat youth. He'd just been taken down a peg by a sassy ginger rocking her flour-stained jeans.

Nearly a half hour later, Natalie was fairly certain her stomach had more fizzing going on than the air bubbles in her likely overflowing dough back at the bed-and-breakfast.

Max St. Cloud was a man. All man. A testosterone powder keg of sexuality. And after over a year of abstinence, her sex-starved body couldn't help reacting. Her military husband had died a year ago, and he'd been deployed to the Middle East for eight months when he died in an explosion.

Still, though, while her B and B, the Cimarron Rose, might be open to the public, her heart was officially closed for business. She was one hundred percent devoted to carving out a life for her and her two children. Colby and Lexie were her world now. They'd suffered too much loss and change. She owed them stability.

The insurance money had just barely paid off their debts.

Her husband had left behind an overextended double mortgage on their home in North Carolina. Doctor and therapist bills for her special-needs son were costly, but necessary. Working and paying for childcare had stretched her budget to the limit. She'd feared she would have to cave and move in with her parents for her children's sake, and then her late husband's military friend Tom Knox had insisted she move close to his place in Texas so he could help and keep an eye on her.

She hated exploiting his kindness, but truth be told, she wasn't close with her family in her hometown of Phoenix. So she'd taken Tom up on his offer. Her family had never been supportive of her decision to travel the world with her military husband, and they definitely weren't supportive of his back-to-back deployments that left her essentially a single parent for years.

The bed-and-breakfast had been a godsend that just sort of fell into her lap—the former proprietor was an older woman who decided to move to California to be with her daughter and had sold it for the right price. Exactly the amount she received on the North Carolina house.

Since four-year-old Colby had recently been diagnosed as being on the autism spectrum, running the B and B was a perfect fit for being more flexible to meet his needs as well as keeping up with her two-year-old daughter. It allowed Natalie to stay home with the kids and pursue her dreams of designing wedding gowns, and gave her the one-on-one time to work with a trainer for their young golden retriever to become her son's service dog. Miss Molly had the smarts and the aptitude, and heaven knew, Natalie needed all the help she could get.

All of which left little time for fizzy flutters in her stomach for tall, dark and dangerous.

Natalie gripped the arms of the leather chair in the Cattleman's Club lounge. "While I want to help, I'm beginning to lose the thread here on your questions. I feel as if we're covering ground you must already know from your research."

"I'm digging for nuances."

"I don't mean to be rude, but you're a computer techie. Not a detective." Okay, so she'd actually been a little rude, but only to give herself distance from Max and his striking aqua eyes with dark lashes, his dark brown, rumpled hair that her fingers itched to comb through. He was quite simply imperfectly gorgeous. This ex-hacker-turned-billionaire tech genius. Bad-boy brilliant. A potent mix.

"I'm experienced with cyberprotection, so it is a combination of both. Quit worrying about what I need to know. Leave that up to me."

"I just expected this interview to go faster."

"Your bread and pastry dough. Can't it be punched down and rise again?"

Now, that surprised her. Because he was right. "A few more minutes, perhaps. But I need to pick up my children from preschool soon."

He nodded, his booted foot resting on his knee and twitching as he took notes on his tablet. Hiking boots. Expensive, clearly, but worn in. Not worn just for show. "Of course. I'll move this along, then."

The image of those well-worn boots and faded jeans contrasted with the button-down shirt and pocket protector. God, why couldn't life be simple for once? "At least Cecilia, Simone and Naomi—they've gone from suspects to victims. Nothing seems off-limits to this creep in what secrets are revealed. Exposing Cecilia's birth certificate in spite of her closed adoption. Sharing private medical details about Simone's in vitro pregnancy. Then announcing Naomi's pregnancy and stealing her chance to share that special news? It's crazy around here. All of us feel vulnerable."

She crossed her arms against her chest, a poor attempt at a shield from all this mess. Still, it made her feel better, if only temporarily.

"You have nothing to hide."

"Everyone has secrets." And she had so many parts of her past that she wanted, more than anything, to wish away.

"You look pretty squeaky clean on the internet."

Her secrets weren't internet worthy. They just made for grief and nightmares and a difficulty in trusting in picket fences anymore. "Well, having our friends hurt is wounding, too."

"I'm not giving up until this bastard is found and stopped." His large hands clenched into strong fists along the arms of his chair.

Very large hands.

Lord, she didn't want to think about clichés about the size of hands and feet right now. She kept her eyes firmly off his boots, damn it.

But the way those hands then unfurled and carefully handled the thin tablet had her envisioning nimble touches and more…so much more.

There was no denying the conviction in his voice, and she couldn't help admiring that. He truly was here to help, and her adopted town needed that help. The people here deserved the best. They'd done so much for her, welcoming her and her children with open arms. She should be helping rather than being so caught up in her own concerns.

This town had welcomed her wholeheartedly and she wanted to feel a part of things, to make a contribution however she could. And she really only had one thing to offer.

She tipped her chin and, before she could change her mind, blurted, "Mr. St. Cloud—um, Max—you can stay at my B and B free of charge, as my thanks for helping out the town."

She might not have as much as some residents of this wealthy town, but she had her pride and she could offer something to help out Royal in its time of need. She was *not* going to fall victim to some smooth-talking player. For the next few days—or even weeks—she could hold strong.

Besides, it wasn't like she was his type of female.

"Thank you very much, Natalie. I will gratefully accept."

He smiled.

And holy hell, that gave her pause. His smile lit his eyes and made her stomach flip in a way she'd forgotten was possible.

What had she gotten herself into?

Cell phone in hand on his way to his rental vehicle, Max charged through the Texas Cattleman's Club parking lot. The old-world men's club dated back to around 1910, and was a large, rambling single-story building made of dark stone and wood with a tall slate roof. He needed to touch base with Chelsea and report on his progress with interviews this afternoon.

And let her know he wasn't going to be staying with her after all. He'd made—his mouth twitched—alternative plans. He unlocked the rented Lexus SUV—a larger car was a must to transport his gear.

Natalie's offer had stunned the hell out of him, but he hadn't even hesitated. Would seducing a suspect jeopardize his investigation? Sure.

Lucky for him, she wasn't a suspect.

Thumbing speed dial for Chels and setting the phone for hands-free talking, Max steered past the stable, pool and tennis courts, all TCC member perks. And all freshly maintained. Chels had told him part of the clubhouse roof and many of the outbuildings had been damaged in a massive tornado a few years back. The group now took special care to reinforce the roof and had added some height to the ceilings so the main building seemed airier than before.

For a club steeped in tradition, a lot had changed in the TCC lately. He might not be a member, but he'd done his research since this group seemed to be the focus of the hacker's attacks. Colors had been brightened. It wasn't such an "old boys' club" anymore, especially because women were now full members.

He accelerated out of the lot and headed toward town, toward the B and B, just as Chelsea answered his call.

"Max!" Her voice chimed through the car's speaker as he drove. "Hello, my friend. How did the fact gathering go after I left?"

"Interesting… Nothing conclusive yet, but lots of pieces to review and leads to follow once I get my gear set up." He'd come straight from the airport.

"I can't thank you enough for dropping everything and coming here personally to help."

Chels's voice filled the car as he made his way down the road. His eyes darted from the asphalt in front of him to the dusty town.

"That's what friends are for. We go way back. I still owe you for teaching me about which fork to use," he joked, tapping his brakes to let a minivan out of a parking lot. She'd taught him more than that. She'd helped him learn the nuances to moving in circles of society he needed to build his business.

She'd also given him the nod to be himself and not let those societal boundaries contain him. Heaven knows, she was an edgy original herself. They really could have been siblings, as they were made from the same mold in many ways.

Slowing, he drove past a school yard teeming with children living idyllic lives of normalcy so different from his. Adults rushed to organize their students into an efficient line for parent pickup. Each little face trusted that their parents or a car pool member would arrive right on cue.

Even from a passing glance, he saw the effort it took to contain the wildness of the children bursting with excitement to return to their home lives and after-school activities—activities that did not include Dumpster diving.

"But you surely have higher-paying clients—especially since you're doing this pro bono, in spite of our offers." She exhaled a hard sigh and he could envision her shoving back her thick honey-blond hair impatiently. "And this feels, perhaps, below your pay grade. You could have sent one of your staff."

"This is sensitive. The info this bastard is sharing hurts you and your friends. I trust my staff, but I don't want you exposed any more than is needed." The criminal had made this personal by launching slanderous attacks on Chels's friends here. Someone had infiltrated their personal data and found dirt for blackmailing—everything from revealing a man's love child, to concocting the appearance of an affair to destroy a marriage, to dabbling in land documents to threaten land holdings. Nothing was secret or sacred to whoever had it in for the people of this town.

Anger rippled through Max as he turned off the main road, eyes squinting in the glare of the September sun.

"Thank you." Her voice wobbled, full of emotional

appreciation. She'd always hated to feel like an imposition, and he never wanted his old friend to feel that way.

His pal had always been an in-your-face, indomitable spirit, ready to kick ass for a cause one moment and outrageously issue a skinny-dip dare in the next. That someone had his friend so afraid and off balance... pissed him off.

"No thanks needed, Chels. I'm here for you, and I'll do whatever it takes to see this through."

"You're a good friend. I look forward to catching up with you while you're staying with me." Even over the phone, he could picture her smile. Loyal. Genuine.

And now he had to figure out how to tell his pseudo sister that he'd made other arrangements for his stay in town.

"Um, about that. I really feel bad about putting you out, so I made arrangements to stay at this nice little B and B called the Cimarron Rose."

Silence stretched for a few heartbeats.

"That's Natalie Valentine's place. You interviewed her today after I left, right?" Her question came out quiet, noncommittal.

He couldn't get a read on her—was she defensive or enthusiastic? Chels wasn't usually guarded around him, so she must be fishing.

Well, he wasn't feeling the need to share about his attraction. While Natalie might be new to the area, it was clear she'd become the town darling. The small community had embraced the young widow, and he sure as hell wasn't the boy-next-door type of person. "Yes, I spoke with Natalie Valentine today. That's how I heard about her place. It seems like a solid fit for me, given I don't know how long I'll be here." He'd done some additional online digging into her business after Natalie left. More detailed, yes, more personal.

The house was a far cry from the penthouse hotel suites he usually frequented. The B and B looked cozy—it was a white wood home, with large porches, ferns and rocking chairs. The ancient oak spread welcoming branches casting long-reaching shadows.

And it was as far from the harsh streets of LA as he ever could have imagined. The town sprawled, buildings seemed to resist the urge to converge, to press against one another. There was space here. Places to go and exist. Places to hide, too.

"Okay, that's cool, Max," Chelsea said slowly.

"You aren't going to argue?" he asked, surprised. "That's a first."

"Nice. Not," she joked right back.

"I would just expect you to warn me off her, given you know who I am, how I am. She's a war widow with two children."

"Of course I know you. Very well, in fact. And I know someday you'll stop running."

Unease crawled up his spine. "Are you trying to push me toward her? Matchmake?"

She chuckled lowly. "I wouldn't dream of maneuvering your life."

Yeah. Right.

Staying silent, he kept on driving, noting the old 1960s' tin diner on the side of the road. A mix of old, rust-peppered cars were scattered throughout the parking lot, contrasting with newer, sleeker models. He had to be close to Natalie's place. Based on the concentration of buildings—the diner, a strip mall and a grocery store—he guessed this was the center of town.

"Max, really, I just figured you must be drawn to her

if you're staying there. You have to admit, that isn't the kind of accommodations you usually choose."

True, perhaps. But there was a time he would have considered the Cimarron Rose pure heaven and far out of his reach. In many ways, it still was. He'd chosen a different path for his life. Impersonal. Sleek.

Impenetrable. Just like his cybersecurity.

So how to deal with Chels's Cupid leanings?

Don't even take the bait. This was about him and Natalie. And who the hell even knew where it might lead? But he wouldn't want there to be gossip. "Natalie offered." Remembering that moment pleased him. She had seemed to surprise herself with the offer, but she'd been sincere. Hell, something told him she'd needed to make the offer and contribute to keeping her town safe. He liked that. "She seems to want to help. I'm comfortable with the choice, and it will give me the opportunity to get the pulse of the traffic flowing in and out of town in a way I wouldn't be able to do staying at your place."

"Right," Chels said skeptically. "Okay, so you're staying there because it's comfy. Got it. Are you sure there's enough bandwidth for you there?"

As if he would rely on anyone else's connection?

"Ah, come on, you know me better than that. Since when do I travel without remote-access capabilities?" He had his own equipment and boosters up the wazoo.

"Okay, I'll be frank. I know you too well to buy these cagey answers. Natalie is not the kind of woman you usually pursue, so I think you need to be careful, for your sake. I care about you, bro." Chels always had a knack for being blunt, even when Max didn't want to hear it.

She was worried about *his* feelings?

For real?

"Who even said I'm chasing her?" he asked too quickly. Damn it. Still, he wasn't giving ground. He pulled into the B and B's lot.

No. This wasn't the kind of place he typically stayed in. The pictures online hardly did the place justice.

The white cottage with reddish-brown trim was framed by an oak tree that seemed to use a tree branch to gesture invitingly to the front door. A warm glow emanated from the windows.

His eyes were drawn to the side yard—to Natalie. A golden retriever danced around, nuzzling Natalie's son. Her daughter stood leaning against her leg, head thrown back in a giggle, red pigtails dancing.

"I just said I'm staying at her place. In fact, she generously offered a room to thank me for helping out with the investigation."

"Uh-huh, okay, Max..."

The rest of his friend's words droned in his ears as he couldn't tear his eyes off Natalie. She'd exchanged her flour-flecked clothes for a simple, long sundress that grazed her curves. She was still earthy but fresh, and her hair swung free.

As if she could tell he was entranced, she turned, looked straight at him. His breath caught in his chest. Like a fist right to the sternum. There was no denying the impact.

He turned off his car. "Chels, I gotta go."

Time to check in to his new digs.

And check out his new landlady.

Two

Concentrate, Natalie sharply reminded herself, looking into the dark eyes of Miss Molly, the golden retriever puppy who had a very specific purpose within their family unit. Natalie wanted to make sure her autistic son had every advantage in the world. And so she'd hired a trainer to help transform Miss Molly into the model service dog. Miss Molly had a lot of potential to help her son.

But not if her mind kept wandering during training sessions like this. Max's handsome face drifted in and out of her mind. He'd unnerved her, caused a rupture in her day-to-day routine—a routine she had carefully constructed since losing her husband. The daily structure was everything she had—it gave her a sense of stability and power.

Enter Max. A big, bad, devilishly handsome tech billionaire. So much for humdrum. For a moment, Natalie couldn't believe she'd offered for him to stay at the bed-and-breakfast. Under her roof. She took a deep breath, pushed him from her thoughts and tried to mirror the movement Margie, Miss Molly's wiry dog trainer, was making.

The sound of an SUV engine mingled with Lexie's giggling at their golden retriever's head tilting at Natalie's command. Lifting her eyes to the road in front of her, she saw him.

Max St. Cloud.

Even from their limited interaction, she'd recognized his features. The door of the black SUV opened and he slid out. His booted feet thudded on the ground, causing dust to encircle him ever so slightly.

Colby nudged her with his foot, causing her to stop gaping for a moment. Her son didn't look at her and didn't touch her outright, but instead kicked the ground with his sneaker, and fidgeted with the plaid shirt he wore.

As if sensing his unease, Miss Molly bounded over to him, planting a wet kiss on his cheek. He smiled slightly, but lines of caution still colored his stance.

Margie knelt beside the dog and Colby. Her sharp blue eyes looked up to meet Natalie's. "New guest? The cyberdetective in from Seattle, right?"

"Yep. That's him," she answered, taking in his slow, confident gait, the ease and appeal of his plain white T-shirt. Natalie's stomach tumbled. With a deep breath, she smoothed her hair, tried to build the wall back up around her emotions.

He was a boarder.

A guest.

Nothing more.

And the butterflies in her stomach damn well needed to listen.

But what could happen with her kids here?

Nothing. Because they were her whole world.

Her daughter, Alexa, bolted from her side, a flurry of kicked-up leaves trailing behind her. She stopped as Max clicked open the picket-fence gate, her little dress still filled with rippled motion. Lexie pulled on the sleeves of her light jean jacket and smiled at him.

"Mister, wanna pet my dog?" Lexie's spritely voice cooed. She pointed back to where Natalie, Margie and Colby stood together.

Natalie rushed to her daughter, then smoothed back her outgoing child's hair and tucked her close. "Lexie, Mr. St. Cloud has had a long day. He needs to go to his room."

"His room?" Lexie glanced up with wide eyes and long lashes. "For a time-out?"

"No, sweetie, he isn't being sent to time-out. He hasn't misbehaved." Although the gleam in his eyes indicated he was open to the option. "He is a guest and we need to be polite."

"Yes, ma'am." She turned to Max. "You hungry? We got pastry, Mr. Cloud."

Natalie started to correct her daughter and he held up a hand.

"It's all right, Natalie." He knelt in front of the toddler. "I like pastry. I hope you'll save some for me for breakfast."

Margie crossed the lawn to join them and tugged one of Lexie's curls lightly. "Show him to his room, Natalie. I'll keep working with Miss Molly and watch these two."

"Thank you, Margie. That's very generous of you."

A blush heated her cheeks. Margie continually went above and beyond what was required of her during these training sessions. When she wasn't training dogs, Margie was part of a search-and-rescue team. A woman in her sixties, she had spent her whole life helping other people.

Margie waved a hand, a tough hand with a scar she'd gotten from a dog bite long ago. "Go on. I've got this under control."

Natalie nodded, motioning for Max to follow her up the porch and into the B and B.

"I'll show you to your room, Mr. S—um, Max." Her tongue had tripped as she remembered he insisted that she call him Max. The lack of his last name made her feel unsettled, put them on a more familiar setting, as if they were old friends or something. As if the boundaries between them were already dissolving...

It was a dangerous thought, one she could not risk.

"Your dog is quite friendly—your daughter, too." The smile in his voice felt genuine as she opened the door to the B and B, the immediate scent of cinnamon filling the air.

She appreciated the homey scent, which grounded her. It was something to focus on aside from the strong male presence beside her.

"I apologize if she talked your ear off." Lord knew, Lexie could talk for hours without much effort.

He paused in the threshold, eyes scanning the area, seeming to scrutinize and process what was before him. She followed his gaze, noting the quirks of this place that she had started to love. Like the wooden knob on the staircase that popped off occasionally. "This is a bed-and-breakfast. I expected the family-style approach."

He clicked the door behind him, making the space seem smaller just by being there.

"I'm curious why you took me up on my offer. Surely you're used to more upscale accommodations," she said, moving through the hallway, her feet soft on the plush vermillion patterned carpet.

"Did you want me to say no?" He cast a sidelong glance at her.

She felt that curious stare even as she kept her eyes forward on where they were going. They passed the door to the bright white-and-yellow kitchen, the room she seemed to always be in. "I wouldn't have offered if I didn't mean it."

They turned the corner and climbed up the second staircase in the house. The stair corridor was lit by sconces on the walls. The bath of golden light always made her think of some grand Regency-era novel. The Cimarron Rose was not the size of an estate, but this particular passage in the house always felt stately, like it belonged as a backdrop for some other time period.

"Do you need the space for paying customers? I don't want to take business away from you." His offer echoed in the stairway, accompanied by his determined footfalls.

They reached the landing and she moved away from him, a fierceness entering her voice. "I have another open room if someone needs to check in."

"I didn't mean to sting your pride." He sounded sincere. He paused again and looked at his surroundings, eyes fixating on a landscape portrait of a sunrise on the plains. Horses darted across the painting, free of all trappings of humanity. She'd bought that painting upon moving to Texas, feeling a kinship with the unbridled herd.

"You're fine. You're just being thoughtful, to me and the whole town. I want to do my part to say thank you and this is the only way I can contribute."

He laughed, a rich sound like caramel. His hand touched her wrist, the scent of his spiced cologne dripping in the space between them. "Then I'll gladly accept the room and the pastries, too."

Her stomach did back flips as she arched an eyebrow his way. "How do you know they're any good?"

"I did my research."

"Don't you let anything in life be a surprise?" She opened the door to his room. Late-afternoon sun streamed in through the old, warped glass window, casting shadows over the bed and threshold.

"Not if I can help it." He took a step closer to her. The light from the room seemed to pierce through his T-shirt, showcase his well-maintained chest. He leaned against the door frame and crossed his arms, the muscles flexing.

The electric pulse of his smile sent her reeling. She watched the way his lips folded into a smile. A spark. No—ten thousand sparks danced in the air. "I need to get back downstairs."

She took a step back, stumbled a little.

"To your children," he said with a knowing look in his eyes.

If she just leaned forward, into him, what would happen? The idea was tempting.

But it wasn't a reality she'd let herself pursue. Natalie straightened, drew herself up to full height. "Actually, the children are with the local dog trainer. She's on the clock." She wasn't going to let this man know how much he'd rattled her. She was a businesswoman. Not as wealthy as him, but her job mattered, her life was full. "I need to return to my customers. Let me know if you need anything during your stay."

A flame lit his eyes.

Ah, hell. She hadn't meant it that way. Or had she?

Either way, she needed to shut up, now, and put some distance between herself and this muscle-bound distraction.

Dropping to sit on the edge of his overstuffed king-size bed, Max surveyed the room. Over the past few hours, he'd transformed the space into a makeshift computer lab. The oak desk, which originally had a globe from the early 1900s, a stack of old novels and a vintage-inspired notepad on top of it, along with three screens, a mouse, a hard drive and an elaborate, curved keyboard. Nothing was plugged in yet, but the layout would do.

He stood and pulled out an array of wires from one of his bags. Crawling beneath the oak desk, he began hooking up the system, determined to catch the creep who had dared go after Chelsea's friends. After setting up the cords, he slunk into a plush leather chair and turned on the computer network system. An array of muted dings and computer groans greeted him, making his room in the Cimarron Rose feel a bit more like home.

While he waited for the remote access to connect with his home system, he spun around in his chair. The cream color of the walls made the room feel cozy, especially with the rich browns and oranges that made up the decor. A vintage map of the world was sprawled above the four-poster bed, and other travel accents—an old camera, repurposed suitcases—punctuated the room.

He glanced at his watch and was shocked. Somehow

the setup of his mobile workstation had taken him a few hours—it was nearing midnight. He needed to stretch.

Pacing around his room, he made his way to the far corner to the window. He scanned the area, noting the play of shadows in the yard...and someone on the wrought iron bench beneath the oak tree.

Natalie.

Natalie beneath the tree with a glass of wine looking as relaxed and natural as a wood sprite.

There. That was his opening. She sat under the oak, her strawberry blond hair soaking up the moon glow. Serene and unguarded. Filled with an urgency to talk to her, he started down the stairs.

Careful to close the door behind him without a sound, he strode toward her, his feet drawn to her before he even figured out what the hell he was doing here. "Do your guests get wine?"

A smile formed on his lips as she turned to find the source of his voice.

She tilted her head back and forth, an exaggeration that exposed the length of her neck and the grace of her movements. Eyebrows raised, she looked at him and lifted her glass. "I'm not sure my grocery-store vintage is up to your elite standards."

"How do you know what my vino standards are?" he returned, just as playfully, taking a seat next to her.

Natalie pursed her lips, folded her legs into the lotus position and turned to face him on the bench. "Seriously? Someone with your income?" She took another sip and held her glass up to the moonlight as if to examine its nuances. "You wouldn't pick this."

"Maybe it wouldn't be my first choice, but that doesn't mean I wouldn't enjoy a glass. Well, unless maybe you have beer instead."

She laughed softly, lowly. "I guess I did offer you a place to stay as my part of thanking you for helping with this cyberwacko." She started to push herself up from the bench. "I have four left from a six-pack of beer in the fridge. It was for Tom Knox when his family visited."

He put his hand on her wrist. "You don't need to wait on me. I can get my own beer. If you don't mind me reaching around in your fridge, that is."

She sank back down. "I'm more than happy to rest my feet."

Max went back inside to the kitchen. The cabinets were painted white, a vibe reminiscent of the 1970s. A beautiful orchid was placed on the kitchen table—vibrant violet.

He made his way to the stout yellow fridge and popped it open. An array of juice boxes and snacks covered the shelves. After some shuffling, he found a beer and headed back outside.

Earlier today, covered in flour, Natalie had been enchanting. Sitting beneath this tree, drenched in starlight and moonlight, she was ethereal. Her hair, loose, natural, rested elegantly on her slender shoulders.

Damn. He should have gotten two beers. No going back now. Opening the bottle, he sat down next to her. She lifted her glass and he clinked his bottle against her drink. "Cheers, Natalie. To solving a mystery."

"To altruistic millionaires." She laughed, then sipped her wine.

Billionaire. But he didn't think that would do much to advance his cause of getting closer to her.

Was that what he was doing?

Hell, yes, he wanted to taste her. Right now he wanted to kiss her more than he wanted...anything.

He took a swig of his beer, the hoppy flavor settling on his palate.

In this moment, underneath the stars and tree limbs, Natalie seemed so easygoing, so much less guarded than she had that afternoon. "Glad you found your brew."

"It was tough at first, tucked behind the juice boxes."

She laughed, choked a little on a sip of wine, then pressed the back of her wrist to her mouth. "Sorry about that. I should have warned you."

"Not a problem. You're a mom. I figure juice boxes come with the territory." Natalie just nodded in response, staring out toward the road.

A night orchestra filled the space between them. Low chirps of active crickets, the occasional rustle of a slight autumn wind through the branches. In the distance, he could hear car tires rolling over the mixture of dirt and pavement. No wonder she liked this time of night. "Your kids are cute. Your daughter sure is a little chatterbox."

"I think sometimes she is filling in the blanks for her brother." She stared into her glass, lightly swirling the wine along the sides of the crystal. "My son's been diagnosed on the spectrum for autism."

"I'm sorry." Her sudden desire to share this private moment struck a chord with Max. As if by instinct, his hand went to hers and he squeezed it reassuringly, noting the way she squeezed back. Max brought his hand back to his side, aware of the absence of warmth.

"I'm just glad we got the diagnosis. Early intervention is key to giving him the most life has to offer. Actually, that's true for any child. Proactive parenting."

"And you're doing it alone."

"I am, which doesn't leave me any free time. You need to understand that."

"You're a superb mother. You don't need to ever apologize for that." Another swig of beer. As he swallowed, he tried to push his own childhood back to the dark morass of his mind. When he was six, his mother had abandoned him. No explanation. Just gone. He became yet another child of the foster care system, cycling through homes, but never finding a permanent place. Never finding a family of his own. Unadoptable. All these years later, the label and reality still stung.

"We're training Miss Molly to help Colby in a number of ways." She combed her fingers through her hair as she turned to face him.

He shifted to face her, closer, as if the rest of the world was outside their pocket of space here. "Like a service dog?"

"Eventually. Right now she would qualify as an ESA—emotional support animal. However, there's no public access with that, but Colby's doctors can quantify how she helps ease his panic attacks. With training, we hope to hone that to where she can assist him in school, the store, and make so many more places accessible to him. My son is also quite the escape artist, so it helps having Miss Molly stick close to him. She barks when we call, even if he won't answer."

"I don't mean to sound dense, but why not just get a dog that's already trained?" Parenting, along with the world of disability and service animals, felt like a foreign language to him, but he was eager to learn more.

"The waiting list for most agencies is one to two years, if they'll even partner a dog with a child as young as Colby. Few groups will. We didn't have a lot of options left to us in this arena." He took in the slump in her spine, her downcast eyes and the pain pulsing in her tight-lipped smile.

He scooted closer to her, raised her chin. Shining emerald eyes met his, and a deep exhale passed from her lips to his receding hand. "But you investigated. You found answers."

Natalie the fighter. Natalie the woman who didn't quit. He admired that.

"Of course. We worked with the trainer and with Megan at the local shelter. They were fantastic in identifying a dog with potential for the job."

"That's impressive."

She worried her bottom lip with her teeth. "There's always the chance Miss Molly won't be able to complete the training to the level we hope. That's a risk with any dog in training. But we're already getting some help with Colby now in the way she offers comfort and sticks close to him. And we're committed to keeping her regardless of how far she progresses in her ability to learn."

"Even if you have to start training with another dog?"

"Yes, even if. For now, though, we're taking things a day at a time, doing the best we can." A stronger, more resolute smile formed on her face, as if she was replaying some scene in her mind.

"You're doing a damn fine job now," he affirmed before taking another sip of his beer, listening to the continued sound of crickets.

"Miss Molly already passed her Canine Good Citizen test. We're not taking this lightly. It's against the law to pass off a fake service dog."

"I didn't say you were." Max stretched his arms, expanding his chest, and let out a low sigh.

"I'm sorry to be defensive. People understand Seeing Eye dogs and dogs that assist with mobility. But when the animal is helping with developmental or emotional disabilities, people can be incredibly…rude and unenlightened." Just as before, Natalie's gaze turned downward, pain evident in every part of her.

"Then enlighten me." He tucked the loose strands of hair behind her ear.

She angled her head away. "I think we need to be careful here."

"What do you mean?" he asked, wanting her to spell it out. What they were feeling.

"I didn't invite you here as anything but a guest."

"Understood."

"An attraction is just that. An attraction. It doesn't have to be acted on."

"Fair enough." He rested his elbows on his knees, clasping his bottle, retreating for now. But only to regroup. "I appreciate your generosity with the room. Your place here offers a homey feel I don't find often in my travels. Now back to talking about your dog. I want to know more about the training."

Even in the moonlight, he noticed a blush rise on her neck. She sipped her wine, before talking into the glass. "You're just being polite."

"I'm curious. Explain it so my techie mind understands."

"Okay, have you heard about studies on dogs that can sniff out cancer?"

"I have." He nodded, gesturing with his beer. "I assume it's like drug-sniffing dogs."

"Nice analogy. And there are dogs that alert to seizures and diabetes glucose drops."

"Keep talking." He genuinely wanted to know. And God, he also liked the sound of her voice.

"Those all involve chemical changes in the body, with physical tells. Think of processing issues and stress from autism in the same way. We can teach the dog to anticipate problems, assist in managing the environment... Your eyes are glazing over."

Narrowing his gaze, he processed the implications of what she was saying.

"No, I'm thinking. It makes sense." He leaned forward, looking past her, eyes alert on the surrounding area, always looking and observing. A calm street in a calm town, no threat to either of them present here. Old habits stayed with him, probably would forever. Including his drive to help, which was giving life to a deep protectiveness for this woman carving out a life on her own in the face of challenges that would have caused many people to crumble. "Have you got an online presence to chronicle your journey with Miss Molly and Colby?"

"In all my free time?" she asked drily.

"You could make a difference for others. Let me help set something up for you. I can make it very user friendly. And you would be surprised at the reach you can get with adding in guest bloggers like your trainer, your vet, people here in town." He grinned. "The cyberworld isn't all bad, you know."

"Why would you do that for me?" Her slender fingertips traced the rim of her wineglass, and she tilted her head in wonderment.

"Because what you're doing is important. You wanted to help. I like to help. I'm a lucky man. I can do what I want with my time. No worries about income. It's not a huge sacrifice really. I'll get one of my techs to work with your trainer. Free publicity for her, since she's volunteering her time at a discount to you. Call it paying things forward."

Her eyes lifted in surprise. "That's really kind of you. Thank you."

A crooked smile spread across his face. "I'm not doing it just to be kind."

"Then why are you?" She leaned into him, desire flashing in her eyes.

"It's a good thing to do..." He angled closer, unable to resist. "And because I really, really want to get on your good side so you'll let me kiss you."

Three

Determined to put a hint of space between them even if she couldn't will herself to just walk away, Natalie flattened a hand to his chest.

The hard, muscled wall of his chest.

Gulp.

"I'm complimented you want to kiss me, but that's not included in the bed-and-breakfast package."

He chuckled, the rumble of his laugh vibrating against her hand. "That's the nicest put-down I've ever received."

Gaining strength, she let out her own low laugh, arching her eyebrows, taking him in, trying to focus on the crisp September air instead of his musky scent. Or the way the shadows played up his bad-boy mystique. "I imagine you don't often get told no."

"Another compliment. For someone who is rejecting me, you're doing it very nicely." Voice still throaty, he swallowed, eyes fixed on hers.

"So you hear me saying no to your advance?"

He shook his head, the line of his lips growing taut. Sincere. "I hear you. *No* is *no*. I just want you to remember I still feel the same way. I want to kiss you. Very much. And if you decide you want to act on this attraction, I'm not going anywhere anytime soon."

The courtyard dimmed ever so slightly. The moody stars seemed brighter as the lights from the B and B went out one by one. People were making their way to bed. She ought to be moving in that direction, too. Away from Max. Away from the way his aqua stare sent her reeling.

"You assume the attraction is mutual." A lame defense. She knew it as soon as the words flicked from her tongue into the night air.

He stayed quiet and held her gaze.

She sighed and rolled her eyes. "Fine. Attraction exists. But I think it's fair to say people don't act every time they're attracted to someone." She looked past him, toward the street. A neighbor walking a border collie shuffled by in a half daze. The sound of gravel shifting beneath paws and feet gave her something else to focus on besides the tempting muscled man in front of her.

"Touché."

"You're conceding?" Narrowing her eyes, she tucked a few strands of hair behind ear, unconvinced.

Max passed the now-empty beer bottle from hand to hand, the green glass glinting. "Not giving in. Just noting your point, since you noted mine. We are attracted to each other. I consider that a huge win. I'm a patient man, especially when the stakes are important." He leaned forward, a devilish twinkle in his eyes. "Very important."

"A kiss? Really?" She'd never met a man patient for a kiss.

He leaned close, so close his breath caressed her face. "Yes, really. What I believe is going to be a *really* amazing kiss."

He smiled at her, collecting his empty bottle and her glass as he stood. His absence allowed for the light breeze to brush her exposed skin, leaving her aware of just how close they'd been sitting. How easy it would have been to act on any of her feelings and temptations. How she simply could not allow herself to do that.

As if she needed another reminder. Watching him walk back to the B and B, Natalie swallowed hard.

Just a boarder. Maybe if she repeated that enough times, it'd be true. Glancing up at the muted stars, Natalie realized it would be quite some time before she would find sleep.

Next to the kitchen, the craft room was Natalie's favorite place to spend time creating—everything from her dresses to accessories she sold in The Courtyard. The little artisanal mall was a big hit in town, and a nice source of extra income for her stretched budget.

She knew she was lucky to have a creative outlet that blended with her life as a single mom. In a house drenched in color riffs of reds and yellows—remnants, in some ways, of a Texas sunset—the craft room boasted a lighter, airy setting. The light sea-foam-green wall stood in contrast to the other cream walls. Tufts of tulle, lace and silky fabrics huddled in the corner, sparking whimsy into Natalie's life.

She ruffled through the half-finished sketches of bridal dresses on the glass desk rimmed with gold, nearly knocking over the arrangement of blue hydran-geas—her favorite.

The room itself, such a stark contrast to the rest of her house, made her feel like she'd stepped into a fairy-tale land. A place outside the reality of her existence. A place where she channeled the grief of losing her husband into more productive, selfless endeavors.

Like running a small, custom-wedding-gown business. Sewing was threaded throughout her entire life for as far back as Natalie could remember. Great-grandmother Elisa had taught her to crochet, and after that Natalie found the act of creation comforting. She'd soon transitioned into sewing, sketching and eventually designing her own clothes.

Natalie had always found art in these moments of baking and sewing. These weren't merely goods to be sold, but pieces of her soul she sent out into the world.

Turning away from the desk after consulting the sketch, she tried not to think of the man staying in the room above. Focus on the here and now. In a slight state of disarray, she noted the piles of airy fabric in her three sewing machines—evidence of her works in progress. More than just her work, it was her creative outlet. A piece of the world just for her.

In the very back corner behind the white couch accented with gold pillows, where her two friends were sipping mimosas, she smiled at the completed gown—a wispy lacy dress with a sweetheart neckline. Perfect for a boho bride. Their figures formed a silhouette against the drawn blind to keep prying eyes out. No one needed to see the masterpiece until after it was complete and the bride made her debut.

Even with the blinds drawn shut, an expansive skylight allowed golden September light to wash over the room, adding to the otherworldly airiness.

Sketch in hand, Natalie made her way to the white couch where Emily Knox sat, green eyes rolling back as she bit into one of the apple turnovers. She swallowed and dabbed her pink lips with a napkin, a smile forming on her whole face. "You have outdone yourself this time, Natalie." Emily placed the turnover back down on the glass-and-gold coffee table, her nimble, long fingers finding the champagne flute.

Natalie couldn't help thinking about the drink with Max, how easy it had been to talk to him, to lean into his touch. How quickly he'd filled her home, her thoughts, her life.

Emily took a sip of the mimosa and then raised her glass to Natalie, appreciation radiating from her eyes and her *yum*. After she set the glass down on the table, Emily carefully arranged the knickknacks and uneaten pastries, pulled out her camera and snapped a picture. She fluffed her honey-brown hair, content to review her image. Emily saw photographically, and her ranch-based home provided a continual canvas of inspiration.

"Please. It's nothing." Natalie shoved her left hand into her pocket, searching for her misplaced measuring tape.

"No, honey, this is delightful," Brandee Lawless offered, staring at her reflection in the ornate mirror. Her dress wasn't quite finished.

A pit of guilt welled in Natalie's stomach as she examined the state of Brandee's dress. She was a mashup of the girl next door and a woman who would fight for her ranch and dreams with every fiber of her body.

Brandee was set to marry Shane Delgado, a rancher and millionaire real-estate developer.

The wedding was approaching, and Brandee's dress was more of a suggestion at this point. Classic lines that felt just right for Brandee—and that was about as far as Natalie had this dress figured out. Silk skimmed over a more structured underdress, and while Natalie imagined lace integrated into the design, the exact positioning was still a work in progress.

Brandee licked a hint of cinnamon from the corner of her mouth. "I'm praying Max St. Cloud can find the person responsible for these cyberattacks. It's just…deplorable what this person is trying to do to the people of this town."

Emily nodded, her normally sunny features darkening. "So much hatred in one person. It must be personal, which is scary because if so, the person could be close." Her voice grew taut, as if the words had to climb over a lump in her vocal cords. "But to try to destroy my marriage. How can a person have a vendetta against so many of us?"

The cyberattacker had sent photos to Emily trying to make her think her husband, Tom, was cheating on her with Natalie. Someone had taken photos of Tom helping Natalie and her children, photos so strategically taken one could almost believe he had a second family. Tom had just been trying to help, had been suffering from a hefty case of survivor's guilt over her husband's death. Life had been hard on all of them.

Thank goodness the Knox marriage had survived and was stronger than ever.

Now Emily and Natalie were even friends. Truth was stronger than hate.

Natalie strategically hugged Brandee, careful not to

press any of the loose pins into her. "Let's not allow that awful person to steal anything more from us by taking our joy. We can't stop him or her—not yet anyway—but we don't have to invite that negativity into our lives. There are so many reasons to rejoice."

Brandee nodded. "Did you hear? Nick and Harper's latest ultrasound showed the twins are both boys. It seems like the population is exploding in our little town."

Emily snorted on a laugh. "Isn't that the truth? It'll be your turn, Brandee, soon enough. We need to keep that joy in mind."

"You're right." Brandee smiled widely. "Nothing should taint every *moment* leading up to my wedding." She twirled around on the pedestal, recalling a lithe ballerina. Even in the half-finished dress, she was a swirl of bridal beauty.

Shoving off the couch, camera slung around her neck and mimosa in hand, Emily strode over to them. "Mimosas and friendship and photos. To weddings. And gorgeous gowns."

"I'm sorry the gown isn't complete." Wringing her hands, Natalie stared at the heap of fabric, beads and lace. At all the yet-to-be-realized potential.

"This is a custom job. I understand that, love that and adore the idea of photos of the gown in progress, fittings and changes." Brandee shrugged, another smile lighting up her face, brightening her eyes. "It's a metaphor for life. The joy and process doesn't stop on the wedding day."

The work.

Natalie blinked back tears. Damn it, she usually didn't let her armor crack this way.

Emily glided forward and wrapped her in a gentle hug. "Oh, God, Nat, I'm sorry."

Natalie willed in one steadying breath after another. Comfort almost made it tougher, but she practically shoved the tears back into her body. Another steadying breath, and she patted her way free of the hug. "Please, don't. It's been a year. I'm moving forward with my life. I'm beginning to remember the happy times that deserve to be celebrated."

Her attraction to Max had been a mixture of relief, in that it assured her she was moving forward, and wariness, because now she needed to figure out if she was ready.

Reaching out to her friend, Brandee gave Natalie's hand an encouraging squeeze. "You're incredible."

Natalie choked on a laugh and sniffled back the last hint of tears. "I wish. But thank you. Making these dresses brings me happiness." She didn't need a man— didn't need Max—because she was happy and fulfilled with the life she'd built.

"And about this moving forward... Would it have something to do with Max St. Cloud staying here?" Shifting her weight from foot to foot, Brandee exchanged a glance with Emily, who offered her a mimosa.

Natalie made notes in her sketchbook, not that she needed to, but it was easier than meeting their eyes.

"Why would you say that? He's just a boarder, staying here while helping the town." Natalie worked to keep the heat from rising to her cheeks.

Brandee snorted halfway through a sip of her mimosa. "Seriously? I saw you two out front playing with the kids and when you walked past each other in the hall on our way in here. The two of you all but launch electric static snapping through the air when you're in the same room." She turned to Emily. "Am I wrong?"

Emily refilled her crystal flute. "Just the looks you two exchange damn near singe my hair."

Natalie conceded the obvious, making her way to the sewing machine. "He's an attractive man, Emily." Arranging the material, she began to work, hoping the sound of the machine would disrupt this conversation.

"And you're an attractive woman." She swept both hands through the air to form Natalie's shape.

Clutching satin, Natalie sagged back from her sewing machine. "I'm a tired, overworked mom."

"Hmm..." Brandee clapped her hands together. "Maybe you need a spa day."

Natalie's spine stiffened defensively. "I'm not going to launch some Cinderella-vamp makeover to snag a man."

Tut-tutting, Brandee shook her head. "No argument. I'm going to schedule it for next week. This is for you. Just for you. You deserve it."

Emily smiled knowingly. "And in case you haven't noticed, you already snagged his attention."

Natalie shot to her feet. "I'm going to get us more pastries and something to drink without alcohol."

With quick steps, she made her way to the kitchen, popped open the largest cabinet and extracted an ornate crystal pitcher—her great-grandmother's. Absently, she tossed the already-sliced lemons from the fridge into the pitcher, filled the bulk of the container with ice cubes and added water. As the impact of water caused the ice-cube cluster to melt and disperse, she heard a steady, almost undetectable sound.

The pitter patter of a slight drip. The sink was leaking ever so slightly. Another thing to fix—after she finished this gown session, of course.

As Natalie began to make her way back to the craft room, the scene from outside the oversize window arrested her gaze.

Max.

But not just Max. He sat at the pink-and-white Little Tikes picnic table across from Lexie. Her chatterbox daughter was serving him imaginary tea, and had just extended a feather boa to Max, who good-naturedly rested the bright purple boa on his shoulders.

As Natalie clutched the water pitcher, she swallowed.

Trouble.

Maybe that spa day wasn't what she needed. Maybe instead she needed the frumpiest burlap sack and chastity belt money could buy.

For the past three days, Max had been holed up at the Texas Cattleman's Club. The beginnings of investigations were always the same. A blur of faces, words, files. For Max, the initial phase of the investigation was at once the most frustrating and most fascinating.

All the contingent possibilities took shape before him—the various paths seemed to reveal themselves as he met with the key town players.

Max had to continue to watch how the men postured, wait for nuggets of information to be dispensed. Analyze. Repeat several more times until something like a lead developed.

After a long Wednesday of scanning through the files of the Texas Cattleman's Club, his eyes demanded some rest, craved home.

He corrected himself. He craved his makeshift bed in his transitory space—the theme of his life. Home was never locatable, and this dusty town was not home, either.

Max barely registered the drive back to the Cimarron Rose. Flashes of leaves turning from bright green to yellow and the lack of cars on the road both gave Max a feeling of timelessness. Ironic, considering everything except for this car ride had turned his world on its head. Max's time at the bed-and-breakfast had been a surprise, to say the least. Not just because of a certain auburn-haired bombshell with sweet, sad eyes that melted his soul. But he'd been surprised how drawn he was to two of the cutest rapscallions on the planet as they rode their tricycles and played ball. Max usually avoided interactions with children, but now it seemed he was living under the same roof as two of them. He should be irritated. Or avoiding them.

Not having freaking tea parties, for God's sake. He laughed to himself, recalling the way Lexie had sidled up to him, her invitation to have a cup of tea was the most earnest request he'd ever heard.

Just like that, two-year-old Lexie—who had inherited her mother's eyes—had him, a big, bad billionaire, eating out of her hand in no time. He'd even worn a boa at her tea party, much to Lexie's delight.

It seemed, though, that four-year-old Colby would be a tougher nut to crack. Could a kid that age be brooding? This one was. How much was the autism and how much was the boy's personality? Max wasn't sure, but he definitely had felt an instant kinship with the boy, who appeared to be a tech geek in the making with his video games and his aptitude at the computer.

But the kinship went deeper. Though their experiences were inherently different, Max knew what it was like to always be positioned on the outside of "normal" routines. As he made his way to the door, he found himself wondering what he could do for Colby. He would figure something out, a way to connect with the kid.

Now, though, he was having a harder time processing his reaction to Natalie, and the instant twinge of arousal that kicked through him every time she entered the room. Hell, even when she was bent over her sewing machine working on a new design for a wedding dress. So Max had decided to give himself a breather by spending some time working on the case these past three days.

But for now, there was no avoiding the need to go back to his room to compile his latest round of interviews and some data he'd gleaned from the Texas Cattleman's Club's files.

As he pulled into the parking lot, he noted the stillness of the air, the lack of guests. So many of the guests who had been there over the weekend had checked out, leaving him largely alone in this place.

As he was turning the doorknob, a scream assaulted his ears. Heart hammering, ratcheting into overtime, he dropped his things at the front door, his body posed to launch in the direction of the distress.

Worry coiled around bones, and an unsettling image of Natalie cornered in the kitchen seemed to permeate every nook and cranny of his mind.

But then another sound.

A squeal of wicked laughter. And another. Suddenly, the bed-and-breakfast was filled with the sound of hysterical laughter, emanating from multiple people. Heart steadying and curiosity rising, he followed the sounds.

His inner investigator egged him on.

The squeals and peals of laughter intensified as he neared the bright kitchen.

Nothing could have prepared Max for the sight in the kitchen. Water pooled everywhere on the tile, and more water continued to bubble from underneath the sink, creating a kind of indoor, shallow water park. Lexie theatrically splashed around, combining water stomping with something that looked like ballet. Her laughter and antics even incited the ever-reserved Colby to motion. Miss Molly ran circles around them, barking and wagging her tail in a golden fan.

Natalie's rich laughter warmed the kitchen, made the disaster seem less like a crisis and more whimsical. Water soaked her shirt and her loose hair dripped, clinging to her.

Those radiant green eyes were calm—she was just as carefree as she'd been under the tree several nights ago.

Stunning.

In every situation—flour dusted, bathed in moonlight, drenched in water—Max felt drawn to her.

Intruding felt wrong. He might have stayed at the threshold for ages if not for the thrum of voices behind him.

Glancing over his shoulder, he saw Tom and Emily Knox approach, hands intertwined.

"Oh, uh…hello," Max said with a surprising semblance of manners, since right now he really wanted them to go away.

"Hello, Max," Emily cooed with half a laugh. "We're picking up Nat's kids and bringing them to our ranch. They are staying with us while she gets all this—" she pointed to the water spewing "—under control."

"That's a real nice gesture. It's heartwarming to know that Natalie has such good people looking out for her. Especially in light of recent events going on around this town."

Emily smoothed back Lexie's hair. "We're friends, happy to help however we can."

"So, Max," Tom said with a knowing grin, "you're playing Sir Galahad with the sink as well as the computers? I would have expected you to be over at the Cattleman's Club."

Emily elbowed her husband in the side before turning to Natalie. "Are the kids ready to go?"

"Practically, other than being soggy—"

Emily waved away Natalie's worry. "We have blankets in the car for the seats. It's a beautiful day for opening the sunroof to dry everyone off. No need to waste time or it'll get too close to their bedtime. Wouldn't want to upset their routine."

"If you're sure..." Natalie nibbled her bottom lip before turning to her kids. "You are both going to behave for Miss Emily and Mr. Tom, aren't you?"

"Yes, Mommy." Lexie bobbed her head. "They have cows!" Lexie's eyes widened as she spoke. Colby simply nodded, then picked at his shirt.

"That sounds fun, sweetie. Now, go get your bags with Miss Emily. They're by the front door away from all this chaos." Natalie's children sloshed through the water.

Tom's brow furrowed as he looked at the mess. "Do you need me to stay and help with the sink and water?"

"You're taking my children. That's honestly the best way to help me because I can focus on clearing up this mess."

Max placed a hand on her shoulder. "Tom, I've got this. Thanks, though."

The whole lot of them made their way to the front

door. Tom scooped up the overnight bags. Lexie wrapped her mother in a hard hug, and Colby even leaned into her, shoulder-to-shoulder, before the two children walked out the door with the Knoxes.

Max swallowed hard and scratched the back of his neck, doing his damnedest to look anywhere but at her wet T-shirt. "You've got quite a mess here."

"Thank goodness I'd already made breakfast pastries for the week. We'll all need to eat breakfast picnic-style." She sagged into a chair with a sigh, a wrench in her hand, and glanced out the window. "I'm praying it won't rain."

He pulled a chair to sit close to her, their knees almost touching. "Temperatures are cool in the morning. It will be perfect. You handle everything with ease."

Max stretched his arms wide, and the buttons on his green polo shirt pulled slightly. He'd opted for comfort today. One of his tactics as an investigator was to come across as unassuming—less like a suit. Which was why he'd worn a polo, cargo shorts and boat shoes today. Respectable without any hint of superiority. People seemed more candid with him that way.

"Ease? I don't think so. I'm holding on by a thread, one day at a time." Her eyes seemed to examine something he couldn't.

"I really do want to help."

She shook her auburn hair and sighed. "You're not paying for my plumber."

"I'm insulted you would think I can't handle a simple plumbing fix." He put his hand on his chest for added drama.

"I really don't expect you to fix my sink."

He shoved himself to his feet in a smooth sweep. "Consider it in the realm of driving along, seeing someone on the side of the road with a flat tire in need of help. It's minimal time and the right thing to do."

Standing as well, she eyed him skeptically. "Are you going to wreck my plumbing?"

He laughed. "If I do, then you can let me pay for it. Now, step aside and don't challenge my manhood, woman."

Pushing the toolbox closer to the sink, he squatted down to investigate what was going on. The leak wasn't too bad—it had just expelled a lot of water.

He noted the tools he needed, and she passed them to him. Natalie sat next to him, eyes watching...learning. With every pass of a tool, their fingers would brush. Slightly. Enough, though, to continuously remind him of how damn attractive she was. Of the mutual draw tugging at both of them relentlessly.

Silence had overtaken them. Max cleared his throat, craving the soothing sound of her voice. "No critiques or advice?"

"Nope. You look like you've got it under control." She laughed, silky hands touching his forearm.

"Hmm..." He emerged from under the sink to stare at her, gesturing for her to take a look.

"What does that mean?" Natalie drew closer, looking at the state of her kitchen sink, inspecting his work but not commenting.

"You're a strong-willed woman. I expected your, um, feedback."

"And risk dinging your manhood when you're fixing my sink for free? I'm quite content to pass wrenches on this." She leaned back on her heels, coy and sexy as hell.

"You look hot doing it, by the way." The words tumbled out. But at least he was being honest. Wrench in hand, he went back under the sink to make the final adjustments, drying things off before he sealed up a couple of joints with plumber's tape.

"I thought you weren't going to hit on me anymore. That any further move was up to me."

"I said I wouldn't kiss you. I didn't say I wouldn't try to make you want to kiss me."

Still, the word *kiss* hung in the air, until he could imagine caressing her ear with his mouth as much as his voice. Someday. Yes, definitely someday.

She crossed her arms over her damp chest, over her breasts pebbling from cold—or desire? "And that's why you're fixing my sink?"

He shrugged, biting off another piece of tape with his teeth. "It's a way to spend time with you." Ah, there. Perfect. The sink cabinet was bone-dry, as were the pipes. "And I'm not fixing your sink. It's officially done."

"And is that why you had a tea party with my daughter? To soften me up? Because I want you to know I absolutely draw the line at you using my children to get to me."

He pushed out from under the sink, and holy hell, they were close. So damn close. He tucked a hand behind her neck and looked her directly in the eyes. "I would never, never use a child to manipulate any situation. That's wrong on more levels than I can count. Believe that."

Her eyes searched his for so long he was tempted to talk, encourage her to speak, but God, the chance to touch her, to look into those deep green eyes of hers was…just damn good. So he held on to the moment that was intimate in a way he couldn't remember feeling before with a woman.

Then she nodded slowly. "Okay."

His throat was raw, his thoughts sluggish. "Okay what?"

"I believe you." She touched his temple with the softest fingers, wiping away droplets of water. "Now that we've cleared that up, I think it's time you kissed me."

Four

Natalie had stunned herself with that proposition.

But she wasn't sorry.

And she wouldn't call the words back.

She couldn't deny the truth to herself or to Max. She wanted him to kiss her. She burned to feel the press of his lips against hers. Her body hungered for a man's touch after so long. After all this time alone, however much she yearned for contact, she hadn't acted. She'd resisted. Until now.

The draw to Max St. Cloud couldn't be denied.

Would he question her?

She barely had time to form that thought before he angled toward her. He slid his hand behind her neck, his broad palm cupping the nape of her neck. His fingers thrust up into her wet hair and she felt the tingle all the way to her roots. Her lips parted and…yes.

Max kissed her. Oh, how he kissed her. His mouth

slanted over hers with a skim, then another as he settled into a fit that only belonged to two specific people. A kiss unique just to them.

His tongue traced along her lips slowly, deliciously. And she was surprised at his careful finesse. He was such an immense and bold personality, she'd expected a more...audacious, forceful even, approach. Yet he took his time. Her fingernails dug into his chest and she wriggled closer, leaning into him.

A rumble of approval vibrated in his chest against her touch and she slid her arms around his neck.

As he leaned back against the cabinet, he pulled her across his lap. She held tighter to him, twisting her body to press her chest to his, her legs draped to the side. Max's mouth returned to hers with a soul-drugging allure that seeped into her senses.

Their wet clothes sealed to each other, the heat of him radiating into her already-combusting body.

The attraction was every bit as strong as she'd thought, dreamed, even feared a little. Because she was a mature woman who knew her wants and desires. This level of chemistry was rare.

Incredible.

If one kiss could set her on fire so intensely, what more would she find in bed with him? And, damn, how fast her mind had skated to there, to images of them naked together, moving and pleasuring each other.

Already she could tell from the brush of his hands and his attention to detail in noting what she liked—yes, that pause to kiss along the tender flesh of her neck— that there was a generosity that would bode well in bed.

He seemed to hear and react to her every hitch of breath, just as she went on alert for clues from him. How when she stroked along the edge of his ears he inhaled deeply, a tug on his earlobe... Yeah, he liked that. Although her wriggle in his lap launched an all-out groan from him. And a throb. A hard, steely throb that made it abundantly clear how much he wanted her.

Pulling away from the warmth of his kiss, she rested her hands on his hard chest for balance. The steady rise and fall of intrigued breathing. The warmth of his eyes searching hers.

Desire pulsed through her, enlivening her joints, her bones. She didn't even seem to register the way her waterlogged clothes clung and hung off her body. Barely noticed how wet his polo shirt had become from the press of her body.

What she did notice was the flame in his eyes, the palpable hunger resting on his lips.

She took a steadying breath, attempting as much as possible to collect herself.

Moments of silence ticked by as they stared deep into each other's eyes. She broke the stare, willing her tongue to form words as butterflies rose in her stomach. "Aren't you going to ask me why I did that?"

"Uh-uh." He tugged lightly on a damp lock of her hair, then traced down the length of the strand.

"Why not?" She couldn't resist leaning her cheek into the cradle of his palm.

"I'm just glad you did." His eyes skimmed over her face, as if he was learning and taking in every aspect of her.

Her face. Not her body. And somehow that felt even more intimate.

"Max, this is complicated. Maybe we need to talk—"

"Who says everything has to be analyzed or discussed? This attraction between us just is."

"I don't want you to think it's an invitation to—"

"Shhh. I don't." He pressed a finger to her mouth. "Quit the overthinking. Stop with the overanalyzing. And yes, I understand. A kiss isn't an automatic invitation to sex."

"I know that."

"I wanted you to understand I know that, as well."

She nibbled her bottom lip, aware of the press of her bottom against his thighs even as she remained with her arms looped around his neck in a fit far too comfortable for her peace of mind. "We're talking a lot, considering you said we aren't going to discuss this."

He rested his forehead against hers, their noses close, their breaths filling the thin space between them. "Then let's make out."

"Make out?" Just kiss? Maybe even heavy petting? But no sex? It sounded…appealing and frustrating all at once. She'd never expected to be single and dating at this stage in her life.

"Yeah, make out… Well, not now, exactly, since we're soaking wet." He plucked at her shirt lightly with a familiarity that teased without going too far. "The kids are gone for the evening. Let's put on some dry clothes. I'll take you out to eat…then we'll go park somewhere."

The plan smoked through her mind and curled in her chest with an appealing swish. Still, she couldn't afford to be impulsive. She needed for things to be clear between them. "That sounds like a date."

"It sure does." Clasping her waist, he lifted her and stood in a smooth move. He set her on her feet and kissed her nose. "Wear a dress. I want to pamper you… and see your legs."

Without another word, he sauntered out of the kitchen, his soaked jeans riding low on those narrow hips and drawing her eyes to his fine ass.

Damn. He was so arrogant and sexy...and yes, irresistible.

For the first time since high school, she was going on a date.

Max slipped out of the kitchen, knowing that if he stayed in there to make this next phone call, Natalie would protest and reject his assistance. The water-filled kitchen needed to be cleaned up, and after a quick search on his phone, he had identified a local cleaning service.

"I'm going to check on a lead really quickly, but you should head upstairs and change into something dry," he called from the threshold, gesturing to his cell.

She nodded. "I do feel a little like a drowned rat." Glancing around the floor, she let out an audible sigh. A weary sigh.

All the more reason to make this call.

Making the arrangements to have the kitchen dried and mopped didn't take too much time. Natalie worked so hard—mothering her children, baking, running a B and B and designing wedding dresses—that he wanted to make just one aspect of her life easier.

While he was on the phone, he watched Natalie swish upstairs to get changed.

For their date.

Which he also needed to get ready for. He headed upstairs, phone in hand—multitasking like a pro. A lot had to be accomplished in a short amount of time.

Next on the agenda: dinner reservations at a five-star steak house.

Max shucked off his drenched clothes and ran his hands through his thick brown hair. Going on this date with Natalie had his heart pounding. He grabbed his favorite sports coat—the one he'd bought when his company made it in the industry. The tie he chose reminded him of his persistence, loyalty and dedication. All things he needed tonight.

After getting dressed, he knocked on her door. She stepped out, a radiant whirl in a silky lavender dress, her hair in loose flowing curls. A simple silver chain with a solitary pearl adorned her neck. But most beautiful of all, her chin tipped with confidence that flamed the fire inside him.

Breath caught in his chest, like warm molasses in his windpipe. All of him was warm. Because of her.

Damn. He was in a helluva lot of trouble. "Shall we?" He extended his arm, eager to have her fingers on him any way he could.

With more of that confidence, she met his gaze with sure bright eyes and slipped her hand on his arm. "We shall. Where are we going?"

A low laugh rumbled deep in his chest. "It's a surprise."

Brows raised, she looked at him sidelong, an easy smile tugging on her cheeks. Her smile outshone any makeup or jewelry.

Seeing her happy... Yeah, he could get off on that all night long.

They walked down the stairs to the SUV. The drive wasn't long, not nearly long enough for him to get his fill of looking at her slim legs. But then he wasn't sure how long would be enough soaking in the appeal of her.

About twenty minutes later, they reached their destination—the Society, a five-star steak house Chels had raved about. He trusted his friend's taste would not steer him wrong tonight in his quest to impress Natalie.

He eyed her across the table, the low lighting playing

with hints of gold in her auburn hair. Her body swayed ever so slightly to the riffs of live Spanish guitar as they talked, reminding him of the way she'd moved in his arms during that kiss that had been spontaneous combustion. She had a dancer's grace, a musician's ear for the rise and fall of the notes. It might not be the right time to make a move for sex, but dancing? Yes, he decided he would dance with her, feel her body against his before long.

Meanwhile, easy conversation flowed, about favorite books, movies, foods, recreation… He couldn't get to know enough about her. He certainly wouldn't have expected she was into hiking. He envisioned dozens of places around the globe he would like to show her… with her kids? Hell, sure, why not? He could imagine her and the kids in a private jet, the dog, too, and maybe the trainer as sitter when he and Natalie wanted time alone—

Holy hell.

The thought caught him up short. Who the hell was he to think of himself in some kind of parental authoritative role? He was far from qualified for that job. And he needed to tread carefully when it came to her children, keep things light, not let them get too attached to him.

Or him to them.

This was about Natalie. And him. And exploring the attraction while he was in town. It couldn't be more, for either of their sakes.

Still, even watching her eat was a total turn-on. She seemed relaxed and was enjoying herself as she finished off her caprese salad with Texas goat cheese. And wine. He already knew she enjoyed her wine…

He added hiking through a French vineyard to his list of possible dates. With a wine-tasting dinner after...

Max found himself wondering when the last time she'd been out like this had been. Or out, period. Natalie seemed to give everyone around her comforts, but didn't seem to allow herself to indulge.

And how he wanted to indulge and spoil her.

The table was small, intimate...and probably too tiny to properly house the amount of food they'd ordered. That didn't matter, though. They were together and that had been the goal.

He held her hand, felt the surge of her pulse increase at his touch. A flush spread over her skin, perceptible even in the dim light of the restaurant. Her eyes moved past him, skimming over the decor. The place, to his eye, looked like a living sunset. Stately paintings of the open Texas terrain hung on the walls, candlelight cast orange hues in the space—the feeling of twilight. Like Natalie.

Her slender fingers twined with his, calling his attention fully back to her. To the present. She raised her brows at him, and the strap of her silky lavender dress slid just off her shoulder as she speared a tomato with her fork.

The image sent him reeling. In the flickering light, he felt like he really saw her. Natalie the caretaker, the tenacious spirit. Her soft hair pooled on her shoulders, the wildness of her curls tamed by a vintage hair comb pushing her hair from her face, revealing her slender features.

Normally he charged ahead and ordered for his date, but tonight he'd found himself settling back, daring her to order for them, wanting to hear what she would pick. She chose filet mignon topped with lemon-butter sauce, steamed asparagus and portobello mushrooms. In between all his questions, she'd eaten with relish— she wasn't one of those three-bites-and-leave-the-rest kind of people.

She savored the meal and, God, he found that sensual relish appealing. When she set down her fork with a satisfied sigh, arousal sent a bolt of heat surging, making him hard with desire.

He tempted fate—and his tenuous hold on his control—and took her hand firmly in his. "I've enjoyed this."

She laughed, shaking her head but not pulling her hand away. "Hearing about my favorite color and top ten movie picks? Surely you have more exciting things going on in your fast-paced life. I've researched you, too, you know."

Plates were cleared to make way for dessert. He lost track of the foods they shared and tasted, well, except for the dessert. That couldn't be forgotten.

Huckleberry sorbet and chocolate ganache.

Still holding her hand, he cut into the dessert and wanted to feed her a bite. Someday. In bed. Together. Yes.

For now, he watched her eat. She smiled deeply, eyes fluttering shut as she tasted the flavors.

A crescendo from the live Spanish guitar cut the silence between them. Natalie cleared her throat, her eyes flickering with a hint of self-consciousness. "I've really indulged tonight. Thank you. This dinner has been lovely, truly." She eased her hand from his and sipped her wine. "But I can't help wondering. Why are we out together? I didn't mean to give you the wrong impression with that impulsive kiss. I think one look at me would make it clear I'm not a fling sort of person."

"We're here because I like you and I admire your tenacity." And yes, he wanted to work his way into her bed.

A fling? Maybe. But not a one-night stand. One night wouldn't come close to quenching the fire he felt for her. And he could swear he saw that same fire in her eyes.

"Tenacity?" She twirled the stem of the crystal glass between her slim fingers, her nails were trimmed short and glistening with clear polish. "How do you know so much about me from such a short time?"

"I'm an observant man. I recognize a survivor when I see one." No matter how comfortable he'd made himself, he'd always carry the memories of foster care with him. He'd always recognize the souls that had been tried by fire. For a fraction of a second, a collage of memories pushed themselves on him—the ammonia-cleaner smell of the group home, the nights spent in an alley-way instead of a bed.

"*Recognize?* That's an interesting word choice." She leaned forward, homing in on the one word that betrayed so much about his life. The life he never spoke of.

He was losing control of the conversation. Time to steer it back to her. "Tell me about your parents."

"They've retired in Arizona." Her face closed off, her smile not reaching her eyes any longer. "I was an only child and had an easy, lucky traditional childhood. They love me."

The normal sparkle in her tone was absent, nothing at all like the glimmer when she talked about her children. There was more to this story. Much more. "And...?"

"That's it." She waved away his question.

"There's always more to the story."

Chewing slowly, she set aside her fork, then swallowed and dabbed at her mouth with her napkin. Weighing her answer? "My parents didn't approve of me marrying Jeremy. They didn't want me moving away. They didn't like how much I was on my own with the children."

"That's the military lifestyle."

Shadows shifted through her green eyes, like lush grassy earth being darkened by clouds covering the sunshine. "They thought he should have served his country for his enlistment commitment and then gotten out."

He clasped her hand in his, squeezing lightly and grazing up to her elbow and down again. "I'm sorry they couldn't have been more supportive of your choices."

"Me, too." She watched the movement of his caress along her arm, but didn't stop him. "They wanted me to move to Arizona to be near them for help after Jeremy…died."

The heaviness of her tone gut-punched him.

"Why didn't you?" A bold question, but Max had never been one to mince words or avoid the uncomfortable aspects of life. He wanted to know, wanted to be there for her.

"They want to parent my children, not be grandparents." Her gaze rose swiftly and her throat moved, hard. "And I really can't bear to live my life hearing them say if we'd listened to them, he would still be alive," she said emphatically.

"That's… God, I'm sorry." The words weren't enough. He knew that. It was all he had for her, though.

She shook her head. "Thank you, but no need. The past is the past." She gripped his hand once, firmly, before letting go and leaning back. "So, survivor, tell me about your parents."

So she wasn't going to let his misplaced word go. He would share the streamlined version. Better than the detailed crap, for sure. "Parent. I never knew my father. My mother was a junkie and I went into the foster system young."

"Max, I'm so sorry. I feel...ungrateful for what I had." She looked down at her plate, her hair obscuring her features.

Nope. He wasn't letting her go down that path. His turn to shake his head. "Don't. This isn't about you. This is just my story of how I became me. My mother fought for custody, I'll give her that. But she didn't fight to get clean, so she eventually lost her parental rights. By then, I was too old to be a cute, chubby adoptable baby or toddler. And I was definitely too much of a delinquent pain in the ass to stay in with one foster family for any length of time." He kept a don't-give-a-damn grin on his face, but his voice felt rusty in the telling, given how few times—never, actually—he'd shared so many details from his past with anyone.

"So you went from foster home to foster home until you were eighteen?" She gripped his hand.

"I was in the LA foster system. It's full. I ended up in a group home, which made it easier for me to slip out and do my own thing."

"What was your own thing?"

He grinned. This was the part he didn't mind talking about. This was his moment of rising. The way he'd come into his own. "Computer hacking. Nothing bigtime illegal." For the most part anyway. More like, well, boundary pushing. "I helped people out with cyber and home security, made some money, pulled myself up and out of my less-than-affluent circumstances."

"You're more than a survivor. You turned your journey into something amazing." She set aside her spoon, her dessert only half-eaten, and as if by habit, nudged the plate toward him.

In case he might want to finish the rest?

Had she done that with her husband? Max sure as hell didn't intend to ask and wasn't going to give her time to question the action. He simply dipped his spoon into the sorbet, his eyes on hers. That electric spark was pushing them together.

"Max?" she whispered, her voice husky. "We were talking about you building your business."

He swallowed, and shrugged dismissively. "So I made some money. I was lucky to have a brain for computers."

"That isn't what I meant." Her thumb stroked along his wrist as she studied him through narrowed eyes, her lashes long.

"What do you mean, then?" He clasped her hand in a firmer grip, stroking up to her elbow and then back over the tops of her fingers.

Her throat moved in a low swallow, her chest rising and falling a hint faster. "You've devoted your life to making other people feel safe. That's admirable."

He didn't want her to have any misconceptions about the kind of man he was. "You're overthinking things."

"Or else I'm observant, like you," she said firmly, meeting his gaze steadfastly. Unflinchingly.

Damn, she was amazing. And he wanted her more than… He couldn't remember when he'd been this hungry.

"Well, you can believe whatever you want if it gets me back to kissing you and closer to second base." He gave her his best Boy Scout smile—ironic really, since he'd never been anything close to a Boy Scout. "Are you ready to go drive around the city and find a scenic mesa perfect for parking?"

* * *

Before Natalie could gather her thoughts for a witty answer—and will her jittery nerves to settle—a clearing throat interrupted them.

Natalie glanced over her shoulder to find Sheriff Nathan Battle standing alongside Gabe Walsh, who also happened to have some hefty PI skills that proved helpful with the Royal Police Department on occasion.

"Hope you don't mind if I interrupt your dinner for a moment." The sheriff stood just behind her, his dark brown eyes narrowed, full of intent. The poster child of a man on a mission.

Not that Natalie found any of this surprising. Sheriff Battle, a kind man who'd poured his life into the community, always had a way of strengthening connections in seemingly strange settings. He was devoted to his community in a way that Natalie deeply appreciated, particularly in the wake of the recent cyberattacks by the maverick character.

"Evening, Max. Natalie." Nathan gave them both a curt nod as he approached the table, eyes resting on Max as hard lines formed in his brow. Worry.

Gabe's eyes showed the same concern, although he stayed silent and nodded in greeting.

Natalie noticed Nathan's wife, Amanda, a few tables away, talking on her cell phone, pen and pad in hand. Multitasking. It must be a trait they shared.

Max pushed back his chair and stood to shake hands with Nathan. "Hello, Sheriff. Gabe. What brings you two to our little table?"

Nathan began, "After we spoke yesterday, I had a thought about…"

The conversation launched into cybertech talk that soon turned into mostly a droning blend in Natalie's ears. Her thoughts fell far from the conversation at hand. Instead, she found herself openly surveying Max, and noticed the way the dim light illuminated his dark features. Could shadows really make a man hotter?

An awareness in her stomach—something like butterflies on steroids—answered an unequivocal yes.

Suddenly hungry again, she scooped into the dessert, letting the cooling sensation of the huckleberry sorbet ground her. The bite allowed her a pause—a second of reflection and distraction as she appreciated the fruit and chocolate flavors.

This had been a helluva night.

Natalie had known Max was charming. But he hadn't seemed real. But after tonight, the narrative offered to her... Well, resisting him seemed more difficult. The rawness and pain in his voice had taken him from being an untouchable sexy data analyst to a human.

What in the world was she going to do with their deep discussion? Did it change anything about her situation at home, her responsibilities...her past? And even on a somewhat lighter note, how did she feel about going "parking"?

"We should arrange for..." Max's voice called her back to the present.

She blinked as Nathan's warm brown eyes reflected excitement.

Max angled forward and planted his hand on the table as he became more invested in the case planning. His fingers brushed hers, so close were their hands on the tablecloth. Jolts of electricity spiked through her bloodstream as she thought about the possibility of parking with Max; carefree, romantic, sensual. The drumroll thought of his body touching hers, of his lips... Anticipation blossomed in her chest.

Scooping into the dessert again, Natalie became aware of another sensation rising in her chest. The unmistakable mark of apprehension twined with her previous desire to go for it. Throw caution to the wind if even for a brief time.

It had been a while since she was intimate with a man—well over a year now, given how long her husband had been deployed even before he died. That wasn't quite the total issue, though.

Conversation—deep conversation—had fallen away long before Jeremy had died. True, their marriage had been in trouble. Rocky times were to be expected. Silence had become the language they spoke. Increasingly withdrawn, Natalie had started to feel like she and her now-deceased husband had occupied different temporalities that never seemed to sync up.

Yet somehow tonight, she was reminded of what it was like to be in the same moment. To share. In her gut, Natalie knew the comparison of one date to years of comfortable routine in a marriage was not fair. Not even close.

But the act of exchanging stories tonight connected her to Max in a way that being physical couldn't. The interweaving of past tragedies left her heart raw, scarred from the weight of multiple losses.

And if she reached out again to touch him, would she be able to pull away? Or was it already too late just from that kiss, from being here tonight?

Because truth be told, she feared she might well have already set something in motion she didn't know how to stop.

Five

Clicking her seat belt into place, she threw a glance at Max as he started the engine of the SUV. The luxurious leather seat creaked as she shifted her weight. Loose curls fell into her face as the familiar feelings of nervousness and desire pulsed in her blood. "You were serious about going parking?"

No taming the rampant thudding in her chest.

As he caught her eye, a smile formed on his lips. A devilish one at that. "If that's what you want, we absolutely can. But you'll have to tell me where the good spots are."

He put the car in Reverse, his right arm went to her headrest so he could see as he backed out of the steak house parking lot. Musk and spice emanated from his sports jacket sleeve. A dizzying effect.

Looking shyly out her side window, she muttered, "How would I know? I'm new here."

"Good point." He winked, the SUV lurching into

motion as they exited the parking lot. Silence passed for a moment as he got onto the main road, heading away from the safety and certainty of Cimarron Rose. Of her carefully constructed life and fortress against feeling. He took them north, the lights on the road scattering, allowing the open Texas sky to be punctuated with flickering heavenly bodies.

Clearing his throat, he added, "I actually took that into consideration and came up with a different plan that didn't involve me asking my friend Chels where the great make-out spots are around here."

She folded her arms across her chest, intrigued as hell. "Oh, you did? And what is your plan, then?"

He shrugged, eyes glued to the road. "I thought you might like to go dancing."

Natalie's shock took the form of a head tilt. "Dancing?" She couldn't even remember the last time she'd cut a rug. Years. It had to have been years. Perhaps her wedding...

She silenced the thought. Brought herself back to the present moment. To movement in sync with this man.

Turning his face to her, he flashed a smile and raised an eyebrow. "Dancing can be every bit as...connecting as making out."

Her thoughts exactly. And didn't the thought cause a rush of heat through her despite the perfectly moderated temperature in his expensive car?

"You're really taking me dancing and not going to hit on me?" Based on the look in his eyes, Natalie didn't quite buy that.

He shook his head and threw on the turn signal. "No, unless you tell me you prefer not to dance."

She gripped his hard-muscled arm. "We can dance."

"Are you sure? Do you want to go back to your

place to make out…maybe get away from the crowd at a hotel? Because if you do, just say the word and I will make love to you well and long through the night. But I got the impression that wasn't something you're ready for." He reached to squeeze her hand. A seriousness seemed to wash over his body, and she sat up straighter. "And I want you to be ready."

Gulp.

Words jumbled in her throat as she attempted to formulate her next words. Her next sentence mattered. She needed to be as precise as possible. The pressure of having to know what she wanted made her ribs tight with tension and the weight of her decision.

Yes. She felt attracted to Max. His ease with words, compliments. That ready, lopsided smile that hinted at his mischievous side. And he was damn sexy with his tousled dark hair and bright, inquisitive eyes.

Losing Jeremy had left her raw. Giving herself away to Max would take time. Trust.

But dancing. She could manage that. Dancing could live in a box, be compartmentalized. "I believe dancing is the wise choice. Thank you."

He turned up the heat in the SUV. "Wise. Hmm… Okay, we'll be wise for tonight."

After a few more minutes on the road, Max navigated the SUV into a spot in Jackson's Honky-tonk. After he parked, Max opened her car door, offering a steadying hand as she stepped out into the graveled parking lot.

"This is not what I expected," she said, looking at the building. Even from the car, she could hear the sounds of country music—big guitar melodies and the echo of twangy voices.

A bitter September wind swept through the area,

sending a shiver down her spine, making her step closer to Max. He rubbed her shoulder.

Opening the heavy wood door to the honky-tonk, he whispered, "I'll be fighting off the cowboys who want to steal you away."

"You're such a talker." A laugh formed on her lips as she surveyed the room. Men in cowboy hats led women to the dance floor. Couples shared drinks, clinked beer bottles together.

Dim yellow lights hung suspended from the ceiling over the bar area. The lighting only seemed to deepen the color of the wood, making the place feel out of time, like a relic from decades ago.

"Is that a challenge?" He shucked off his sports coat and draped it on the back of a chair at an unoccupied high-top table. His lips thinned to a confident line.

"All right, then. I hope you are prepared for this." She pulled her heels off, becoming substantially shorter but growing in confidence.

They made their way to the dance floor. Bright spot-lights illuminated the area. She leveled her gaze at him, remembering the times she and her college friends used to frequent a country bar, learning all the line dances and smiling at cowboys. Her roommate, Jessie, made them go week after week. She was a Georgia girl, through and through. Weekly visits had made Jessie feel more at home during that scary time of transition. Natalie picked up the steps to the various dances quickly, found a way to lose herself in the music and movement.

This was her turf.

A square dancing song began and the crowd let out a variety of emphatic whoops. Max and Natalie began as partners, but soon the movement of the dance swept them from each other.

No matter which partner she found herself with, her eyes found Max's. Even from across the room, the stare electrified her.

Eventually, the song ended and he closed the distance between them. Suddenly, she took in how tall he was, noticed how the other women dressed in cowboy boots eyed him. He didn't pay them any mind.

His steady gaze seemed to see her—only her. As if they were alone in this space.

The Texas two-step began, and his arm instinctively went to the small of her back. Taking his hand in hers, they swayed together. Bodies melting into one another.

For four more songs, they stayed like that.

A country ballad replaced the more active tunes. Sweat had pooled on her brow and his. The lights dimmed, became cooler. Natalie's hips swished in time to the slow music. Max's agility surprised her, thrilled her. She pressed closer to his chest, looked up at him.

His lips were so close to hers now. They tasted the same breath.

Max's hand tangled in her hair. He lowered his mouth to hers. A kiss unfolded, exploded her sense of control.

What had started as a gentle kiss soon deepened to pure passion. Electricity still surged and hummed beneath her skin.

Her tongue explored his mouth, drawing them somehow closer together. All sounds seemed to fade.

Nothing else existed.

Except for a faint ringing. A literal vibration.

Her imagination? She felt disoriented at the sensation, distracted by the taste of him.

Slowly, the sound registered. Her phone was in Max's pocket. Pulling away, she said breathily, "I need to take that. My kids…"

Heart still pounding, she waited as he fished the phone out of his pocket. She answered it, rushing off the dance floor.

She'd been too late—no one was on the other line. Stepping farther away from the dance floor, she went to return the phone call. A text buzzed through.

Lexie was crying. She wanted to come home now. Natalie's heart sank. Guilt washed over her. She needed to be there for her kids. Not gallivanting with a mind-numbingly sexy man at a smoky honky-tonk. How could she have thought otherwise for a second?

I'll be there in a half hour.

She sent the text. Max had reached her now, concern washing over his features.

"I need to go pick up my kids." She needed to get her head on straight while she was at it. Remember that she wasn't in a position to indulge herself with a wildly sexy newcomer to town.

He nodded. "Of course." Turning on his heel, he went to collect their things from the table.

What she didn't add—couldn't add—was that she also needed to process this whole night. The moment. The spark.

Everything.

She needed to salvage more self-control before she spent any more time alone with Max.

For Max, the morning crawled. There wasn't a moment that hadn't been filled with movement, but since picking up Natalie's children last night, things with Natalie had cooled.

She'd barely spoken to him.

In her rushed "good morning," he'd felt her defenses reforming. She avoided his gaze, pushed past him and mumbled something about work.

To be fair, Max knew she was an overachiever—a woman pulled in too many directions. Or at least, too many directions for the hours in a day.

Still, after that dinner and the slow dance...the distance felt calculated. Stress radiated from her as she passed him in the hall, making her way to the craft room. He could see it take hold of her shoulders, enter her stance.

She'd served her B and B guests an elaborate spread of a breakfast picnic. Brie cheese, fresh croissants, an assortment of breads, apple turnovers, grapes and strawberries covered the table on the outside porch. The cool temperatures provided an inviting backdrop for guests as they piled fruit and pastries onto plates, grabbed picnic blankets from the stack and arranged themselves on the lawn.

Sipping fresh coffee that she'd also brewed for the guests, Max found himself wondering how she managed all this. Determined to make a difference for this kind, selfless woman, Max put himself to good use. He'd help her out this morning. As guests finished their breakfasts, they dispersed. Natalie had done a quick cleanup before Margie spent some time playing with the kids and dog, canine socialization more than training.

Chaz and Francesca, a young couple Max had met while standing in line for coffee, began looking a little antsy. Francesca's inquisitive brown eyes scanned the area, looking for something. Based on Chaz's glance at his watch, Max surmised they were waiting for Natalie.

Chaz folded and unfolded the receipt, the kind Max

had seen Natalie slide under doors of departing guests each morning.

Rather than disrupt Natalie, he took their checkout form, looked it over quickly and confirmed they'd paid. Nothing more needed doing, no need to get Natalie to run payment. He couldn't help but notice her computer was open, not password locked. He really did need to upgrade her security—internet and building.

After tapping a message into his phone about her system, Max glanced at his watch. It was 11:45 a.m., and he noticed how both Lexie and Colby watched television, sharing a little bowl of strawberries while Miss Molly napped on the floor in front of them. Margie had ducked out a few minutes ago, and asked him to send a shout-out to Natalie. Which he'd decided to delay. He could watch the kids while they sat in front of a television.

And there was another way he could help Natalie, since not many realized he knew his way around a kitchen.

He walked into the common room and stooped to be eye level with the kids. His heart hammered. This was a new space, and part of him couldn't believe how easy and natural this instinct was. But then again, as much as he didn't like to address it, kids spoke to him in a way.

His years in foster care had made him more empathetic, more in tune with what people needed. Max supposed it allowed him to literally see the world differently. To be attentive to details, how people interacted. What they weren't saying. All of this made him a good detective now.

And what he saw when he looked into the TV room was two well-behaved but hungry children.

"Hey, kids," he called out. "Whaddya say we make some lunch?"

Lexie's green eyes lit up as she clasped her hands over her mouth. "Yeah! Yes, yes, please, Mr. Max. You cookin'?"

Her squeals and giggles reassured him that he'd made the right decision. Even Colby nodded, a faint trace of a smile forming as he pushed himself off the big red couch.

The trio made their way to the kitchen. Other guests milled around. Snippets of conversation filled the halls.

"I wub pancakes for lunch." Lexie teetered back and forth as she opened the pantry door, pointing to the pancake mix. She grabbed a jar of sprinkles from one of the lower shelves. "With this, too."

With a light nod, Max picked up the pancake mix, and grabbed the sprinkles from Lexie's extended hand. Not a stretch for his cooking skills, but if that was what they wanted, then he was happy to comply. "What about you, buddy? Do you like pancakes for lunch?"

Colby considered Max's question. The young kid seemed to hold a microscope up to Max, examining him in that quiet way of his. For a moment, Max felt Colby wasn't going to answer him, and he'd learned that sometimes the boy refused to talk. And in those cases, there was nothing to be done to force him. In fact, pushing the issue could cause the child to have a meltdown or retreat into hiding.

Just when Max was about to give up, Colby spoke in a small but confident voice. "Yes. But plain. No sprinkles. Three small pancakes. Circle. But don't stack them."

"Gotcha. Circles. No sprinkles," Max replied, pulling out bowls from the cabinet. He opened the fridge and extracted eggs, milk and butter. He found two pans and started heating them up. "We should probably make more than pancakes, though. Like healthy stuff. Do you like bacon or sausage?"

"Bacon," Lexie said, climbing a three-step ladder by the counter so she could see better. Her blanket trailed from her fist.

"Sausage, please," Colby said, his wide eyes hesitant as if choosing differently from his sister would cause trouble.

And in that moment, Max's gut clenched. Sure it was just bacon and sausage. An easy enough request to fill. Nothing like the tougher stuff of dealing with children—the more intense needs they deserved to have met by responsible adults in their lives.

So he would stick to food, because the Valentine family in this simple B and B was far from simple at all.

Panicked, Natalie rushed into the kitchen, swiping perspiration from her forehead.

It was just past noon, and she didn't know where the morning had gone. So much had to be done, and one of her guests had let her know that Max was starting lunch for her kids. Embarrassment burned her cheeks as she saw the array of cooking supplies Max had gathered.

He didn't have to do that. Shouldn't have to. Damn it, but she was coming apart at the seams trying to manage everything. And that no doubt showed in her appearance.

Her hair was tucked up into a messy bun she would have liked to call chic. Ha. Were snug jeans sexy when they were tight? Because the ones of hers that fit were all dirty. She'd dug these out of the back of her closet, a pair from prebaby days, along with a simple V-neck T-shirt tight around her breasts.

Yet he made low-slung jeans and a soft T-shirt look...yum.

Swiping back a loose lock of hair, she drew in a steadying breath. "I can't believe I worked into lunchtime."

Natalie opened the back door and called to Miss Molly with the proper commands and gestures, sending her into the fenced area of the yard where guests weren't allowed. "I'm so embarrassed and so sorry to have imposed on you." She clasped her daughter by the shoulder and touched her son lightly on the hand, just a fingertip brush. "Let's have some soup and PBJs."

Her daughter's bottom lip quivered. "Want Mr. Max make pancakes."

"Lexie—" Natalie began.

"Natalie, really," Max interrupted. "It's no big deal. Either I can cook for myself here or I'll have to go out to eat, which will take longer. So, free pancakes for me in exchange for my work?"

He was being nice in making this face-saving excuse, but still... She shook her head. "They're children, *my* kids."

"Kids?" He raised an eyebrow, egg in hand hovering over the bowl. "Are you insinuating I can't handle feeding young palates?"

Damn, he was charming. No wonder he'd taken the business world by storm, amassing a fortune beyond anything she could comprehend.

Rich or not, though, that didn't make him the boss of her domain.

She stood her ground. "I'm saying thank you, but I'm not your responsibility. I'll even cook the pancakes and you can have some, since you're a guest—"

Colby pulled her hand. He so rarely touched her any

contact instantly stopped her cold. "Mom, please. Color with me. He can cook."

And oh, God, that tugged at her heart with memories of family meals with Jeremy. She needed to separate the past from the present. And in this present her son's needs and wants came first.

It was just pancakes. And a coloring page. If it made her children happy... "Okay, Max, if you're really sure you don't mind."

The familiar roguish smile returned to his face, sparking him to movement. With a bold flourish, he grabbed a towel, wrapped it around his waist and winked at her. "I don't mind at all. I enjoy cooking, and I travel so much I don't get to do it nearly often enough."

Instantly, the dance from last night rushed back into her mind. How close they'd been. How easily they'd kissed.

Oh, that kiss.

Her knees went a little wobbly and she held on to the table's edge as she sat with her children while Max began cooking. The sound of eggs beating and the soft hum of the oven filled the kitchen, mingling with the sound of colored pencils touching down on paper.

Colby had a blue pencil in his hand and he carefully colored in a large fish—his obsession. Natalie picked up a green pencil and joined her son in coloring, half watching Max move about her kitchen with a smooth efficiency and confidence.

Did the children remember the old days when their father had been home, in the kitchen with them? He hadn't been much for cooking, but he'd played with the kids while she prepared meals. Her gaze skated back to Max.

He managed multiple pans at once. Bacon. Sausages.

Pancakes and even crepes in another. He'd grabbed the leftover caramel and apples from this morning's pastries. He caught her eye and mouthed "crepes for the lady" with a wink in her direction that sent a tingle of awareness along her skin, prickling in her breasts.

She couldn't help it. She smiled. Although she quickly tucked her head to color and tried to hide how far that smile reached, deep inside her. The smells of fresh food—food she didn't have to prepare—felt good. Damn good. This whole moment did and all because of Max.

After washing the pans, he dished up the kids' food and placed it on their small, plastic table tucked in the corner. "Coloring break and time for grub."

Max ruffled Lexie's hair and yet was careful to keep his hands off her son, clearly aware Colby preferred to call the shots on hugs.

Natalie said softly, "Thank you."

For more than the food. For the thought. For being here. For the three perfect, sprinkle-free circles on Colby's plate that weren't stacked.

Max spread his hands. "All under control. And as much as I would like to stay here and, uh, dance with you, I need to head over to the Cattleman's Club to meet with some members."

He started grabbing the cooking supplies to put them away, eyes flicking to the B and B guests that stood at the threshold of the kitchen. She joined him, gathering more supplies in her hands, and they went into the pantry. Together.

Away from people, he set down his supplies, leaned in for a kiss.

A deep body sigh had her melting into him. The

kiss wasn't as feverish as last night, but it was every bit as hungry.

Maybe it was she who was hungry. Despite all her talk about self-control, she allowed herself just a moment to touch him. His strong chest and arms. The corded neck. His warm jaw, where the skin bristled ever so slightly against her palms.

Just one kiss and she felt like she might come out of her skin.

"Why are you pursuing me so?" She eased back to look into his eyes.

Not his talented lips. Nope. Not looking there.

She struggled to catch her breath, and staring at his sexy-as-hell mouth would not help matters.

His eyes narrowed. "I'm not sure I understand the question."

Didn't understand? Or didn't want to discuss it?

For her part, she'd rather lose herself in the feel of his mouth on hers again. The feel of his hands on her waist. Her back. Her everywhere.

But she couldn't go on like this, kissing in pantries. "I'm not exactly your type," she said to clarify.

"Natalie," he whispered into her ear, his breath hot. "Stop with Googling stuff about me and get to know the real person."

Her thoughts scrambled at the feel of his lips against her neck. "I Google everyone who stays here—for safety purposes."

"Sure. You like me, though." He skimmed his mouth back around to hers, his grin decidedly devilish.

Handsome. Hot. Charming.

He wasn't wrong. But maybe that didn't matter.

Still, she felt compelled to repeat what she said. "I'm really not your type."

He angled back to look at her, his expression solemn, as if he sensed how important this mystery was to her. "You're so sexy I've been on fire for you since the second I saw you." He tugged at the loose band holding up her hair, sending it free around her shoulders. His fingers combed through. "That makes you my type."

Okay, that brought another question, perhaps an even more important one. "What if you're not my type? I'm not talking about attraction. I'm talking about type, what's good for me."

Or good for her children. She had to think of them. Especially with Colby's special needs. Sure, Max had figured out not to pat the boy on the head and to keep sprinkles out of his pancakes, but that wasn't the same as dealing with the challenges of parenting a special-needs child day in and day out.

"If you don't want me in your life, Natalie, then tell me to go." Silence hung between them. He nodded once. "And that's my point."

"But as you said, this is about attraction. And yes, maybe I'm attracted to a bad-boy type, and as much as I loved my husband, I'm not saying that marriage or love guaranteed happiness." Concern burned in her belly.

He drew closer, ran a hand up and down her arm. "Okay, so you're saying you don't want a relationship and there's no replacing your husband." He kissed her forehead. "Let's stop talking about types and the past. It's not about trying to logically explain what's happening between us."

"You're a cyberguru. Doesn't that make you the epitome of logical?"

His low laugh rumbled his chest against hers. "I like to think I'm a Renaissance man, in touch with my emotions. I'm here for now. Let's go with the flow."

In the moments before the next kiss, she searched his eyes and wondered if, and how long, she could take him up on that dare?

As Natalie cracked open the door, a long yawn of hall light winked into her daughter's room, illuminating Lexie's sleeping form. At the threshold, Natalie watched the steady rise and fall of her daughter's breathing.

With silent footfalls, Natalie crossed the room, and made it to her daughter's bedside. She planted a kiss on Lexie's forehead. Lexie didn't stir, seemed content in whatever sweet dreamscape danced before her closed eyelids. A small stuffed animal—a unicorn named Mrs. Agatha—was snuggled up next to her daughter, whose little fingers were twined in the purple mane.

Content with the scene at hand, Natalie left Lexie's bedside and made her way to Colby's room for their nighttime ritual.

The last rays of the sun had melted away, and the hall no longer boasted a cool autumn glow. Instead, the manufactured light of the hall—dim in comparison to the natural amber of a few moments ago—guided her to the other end of the hall, to the blue door that led to Colby.

Clicking open the door, she let herself into the plain white room. Paintings of fish lined the walls, an array of end-of-the-rainbow colors dancing before her eyes. She'd made a gallery wall for him—hung up his meticulously colored pages of deep-sea fish. He seemed to enjoy the soothing nautical world.

She stretched, eyes meeting the now-familiar scene of Colby underneath his blanket, reading. He had his own flashlight, one she'd bought him with the barrel decorated in magnifying glasses and microscopes, part of a science kit.

The weighted blanket draped over his head, thick enough to give him the pressure he preferred, but thin enough for remnants of the flashlight's beam to penetrate the fabric as he read underneath. A silent fan whirred, cooling him. Miss Molly was stretched out beside him, pressed up against her charge.

Miss Molly's deep brown eyes seemed to spark with interest as Natalie made her way to the bedside. Tail thumping, the golden retriever let out a small whine but didn't move away from Colby.

He let the blanket slide down, exposing himself to the air of his room and to her. Natalie's heart fluttered a bit, as she wondered how to connect and engage with her son—her deeply kind son—even more.

Hugs were on his terms, but they had developed another language of affection. She softly tapped her fingertips along the top of his hand, then his forehead. A smile pushed up his lips, reached his eyes.

Not a hug, but a connection. A genuine connection. These little moments meant everything to her, and she imprinted them into her memories to draw comfort from in tougher times.

He closed his book and set it aside, then turned off his flashlight as a yawn shook his whole body. Blinking at her, he lay down. "Good night."

So matter-of-fact and confident.

"Good night, Colby." She stroked a hand along Miss Molly's swirls of fur, the dog being the link between them; then she closed the door after her.

She sagged back against the hall wall and let out a hard sigh. Glancing down the hall, she noted—how could she not?—that a warm glow emanated from under Max's door.

He was still awake and here.

Not that it should matter to her.

Still, she envisioned him in the room, casual and relaxed in her home. More than just a guest?

Silly thoughts. Shaking her head, she pulled her phone out of her pocket. It had been a few weeks since she'd spoken to her own parents. An overdue conversation.

Natalie glanced over the railing and down, nodding at the guests sitting in the landing area on an overstuffed couch. They were huddled under a fluffy blanket with the staples of movie watching—popcorn and candy. The thirtysomething man, Albert, balanced a laptop on his lap while his wife, Beth, rested her head on his shoulder.

The thing about running a B and B was that Natalie continually had access to private moments. And many—like this one—made another tear in her barely healed heart. Which made it all the easier to respect the couple's privacy. She went quickly downstairs on soft feet to make her phone call.

Natalie rounded the corner into the kitchen, sat at the table and dragged in a couple of bracing breaths before she hit the speed dial for her mother.

Five rings.

It had taken five rings for her mother to answer. Already, a knot formed in Natalie's stomach.

"Hey, Mom. How are things?" Staring hard at the table and scratching her finger along a scar Colby had worn into the wood with a compulsive scratch when he was three, she waited for her mother to respond.

"Hello, Natalie. It's nice to hear from you after all this time." The dig chipped away at Natalie's heart. "Things are just fine here. Your father and I are planning a vacation."

"Oh? Where are you two going?" Natalie asked, winding her hair around her fingers. Nervous habits died hard.

Her mother, Georgina, let out a long, exasperated sigh. "Clearwater Beach vacation. In Florida. We might as well."

Not a word asking about how her grandchildren were doing. How she was doing. Not that she expected or needed it. But still…

"How's Dad?" Natalie asked, hoping to talk to him. She seldom heard from her father on the phone.

"Just fine. Though we are about to have dinner out on the balcony. Hope you and the kids are well," Georgina said tightly. She'd made it clear long ago that if Natalie wasn't willing to do things their way, then she didn't have their support.

As a mother, Natalie found that tougher and tougher to accept or understand.

"Well, enjoy your meal, then. We can speak another time. Bye, Mom. Love you and Dad." She said it out of habit, but meant it even as she wished for more. God, was she destined to always be wishing for more from people who were supposed to be partners in this life journey—people like her parents, like Jeremy?

"Love you, too."

And just like that, the connection went dead, leaving Natalie feeling hollow and raw.

Lord knew that hadn't been their worst conversation. When Natalie had decided to move to Texas, the conversations were laced with distaste and annoyance.

But things hadn't warmed up between her and her mother. The connection between them felt strained. It always had. So different than the connection she felt with her own children.

The tendrils of anxiety inched around her heart. Restlessness entered her limbs, and she found herself walking back up the stairs, past the couple watching movies, toward her kids' rooms. The lights were still out in Colby's and Lexie's respective rooms. She laid a hand on Colby's door and took a deep breath, vowing to always be there for her children.

As she turned, the glow from underneath Max's door caught her attention.

He was still awake. Still up. And yes, from the rustling sound inside, he was still here.

The prospect excited her. And while life hadn't turned out the way she'd hoped or given her what she might have always wanted, she couldn't control what others did or felt. She only had control of her own decisions and actions. In this exact moment, she knew what she wanted.

She wanted something just for herself.

She wanted to sleep with Max St. Cloud.

Six

His eyes strained while he reviewed the code sprawling on the laptop screen in front of him.

Dissatisfied with the machine language, Max shifted his laptop to the edge of the bed. His hand reached blindly to the wooden end table, and he felt around for the mason jar full of sweet tea. Not exactly a protein shake—his normal ritual—but apparently sweet temptation abounded everywhere here in all forms.

A few hours ago, he'd left the room, needing movement to rejuvenate his senses. As far as the case went, he knew a piece of information escaped him.

That frustrated him. Rather than spend a few hours falling through rabbit holes, Max had changed his environment. Foot-to-pavement time always allowed him to clear his head. Or at least it had.

Every stride he took looped his mind back to Natalie. And while he didn't actively think about the case, he did think about the smile of appreciation she'd given him earlier over pancakes and crepes.

He'd run harder than usual. As if running would not only reveal the origin of the cyberattacker, but also reveal a way for Max to proceed with Natalie.

The postrun shower renewed him. Max had felt ready to dive back into this work. Ready for a break in the case. He needed it, really.

But the backdoor code analysis hadn't revealed anything useful. He blinked, sipping the tea, noting how the cool liquid soothed his throat. Satisfied, he set the tea back on the end table next to the fresh-cut flowers from the yard, a nice touch that Natalie made all around the B and B.

Amazing how often she slid into his thoughts.

Time for another change of scene. He made his way to the desk, leaned against the plush chair. A new angle—one that focused on the members of TCC.

Max ran a hand through his hair, sighed deeply. On the edge of his four-poster bed, just to the left of where he'd placed his laptop, a large spread of papers loomed. He picked up the stack and the laptop, made his way back to the main workstation and settled into the chair.

Ready.

He'd been looking into members who had been outspoken about allowing women in the Texas Cattleman's Club and compiling a list of people who'd been denied membership. Maybe someone had a grudge against members after being excluded. This list was damn long. He would have to farm out some of the names to employees in his firm. Once they found identifying markers, he could dig deeper into the cyberworld and with human intel here.

He leaned back in his chair, the floorboards creaking beneath.

When he closed his eyes, his thoughts went right back to his date with Natalie. Kissing her, the way she felt pressed up against him. How freely she'd given herself over to dancing. No matter how many showers he took, he could still smell the flowery scent of her hair.

A rap on the door forced his eyes open. His heart rate accelerated as he cleared his throat to answer.

He swiveled in his chair and faced the door. "Come in."

Natalie in the flesh, not in his memory. Looking as sexy as ever. Maybe even sexier.

She held a plate with a slice of pecan pie à la mode. A loose cotton dress draped along her curves and brushed the tops of her bare feet. "I saw you were still burning the midnight oil and thought you might like a late-night snack."

Oh, he was hungry all right. Looking at her sent a gnawing ache straight to his gut.

"That's incredibly thoughtful of you."

She stayed in the doorway, not walking in but not passing over the plate. He tried to get a read off her and what she wanted. She scrunched her toes, and he noticed her nails were painted green. Interesting. Not the conventional choice he would have expected.

And damn, he was in a sad shape if he was obsessing over her toes. He scratched his chest over his heavily thudding heart and realized he wasn't wearing a shirt.

Max cleared his throat. "I'll grab a T-shirt and we can go downstairs to get a second slice of pie for you to join me."

Natalie looked over her shoulder at the empty hall

and then took a step closer to him. "How about you leave the shirt off and we share this one in your room?"

Whoa.

Just holy hell, whoa.

That was not what he'd expected her to say.

As much as he wanted to haul her in without hesitation, he was starting to care about her. He wanted to be certain she wouldn't regret this and boot him on his ass five seconds later. "Are the kids with Tom and Emily?"

She held up her phone, a low hum of music emanating. "I have a monitor going between their bedrooms. They're next door. I'll hear if they need me. I figured that out for keeping them safe and separate from boarders."

"Of course. I should have realized you would have that figured out." He didn't know much—anything—about parenting. His mother sure hadn't kept track of him at that age and his foster families were usually overwhelmed by the sheer number of kids around. Natalie was…incredible. Beautiful and giving. He should tell her to go. Should. But couldn't. "Are you certain you want to share that pie?"

"Absolutely certain." She met his eyes without hesitation, and with her free hand placed a condom in his palm.

Not much stunned him anymore.

Well, not until Natalie had walked into his life.

His hand closed around the condom. She couldn't be any more obvious than that.

He stepped aside, clearing the way.

She looked back over her shoulder at him with a toss of her hair. "Aren't you going to ask me why?"

"And give you a chance to talk yourself out of being here? I don't think so." He closed the door with a decisive click. All the doors locked automatically, like at a hotel, an upgrade to the place he appreciated right now.

She glanced at the desk and he nudged aside the computer, clearing a space for the plate. Natalie put down the pie, pulled two spoons from her pocket and held them up. "I'm hoping you'll share?"

"My pleasure." He plucked a spoon from her hand and clasped her wrist in his other hand. "One condition, though."

She tipped her head to the side. "What would that be?"

"We get to feed each other," he said, grinning as he sat and pulled her into his lap.

Laughing, she sat sideways across his legs. She swept her spoon through the ice cream and started toward him, only to snatch the bite for herself at the last moment. Her green eyes twinkled.

He chuckled, surprised at her playfulness. She was always so serious. But then she was always overworked. He'd been drawn to her before. Now he was...mesmerized.

Scooping up a taste of ice cream, he brought the spoon to her mouth and didn't play.

She closed her lips over the spoon and moaned in appreciation. "I'm not being much of a hostess, and this really is tasty, if I do say so myself. The ice cream is home churned."

This time, she didn't play, but offered him a taste with some pecan pie mixed in. He'd eaten at the best restaurants around the world, but damned if he could remember ever having had homemade ice cream before. Either it was the best ever, or being with Natalie made it the best ever.

To hell with food. He kissed her. Really kissed her. And hell, yes, she really kissed him back.

While savoring the taste of vanilla on her tongue, he set aside his spoon with a clink of metal against china and plucked her spoon from her hand, as well. The curve of her hip pressed against him in a temptation even sweeter than the dessert. Having her in his arms was better and better every time.

He didn't know what he'd ever done in his life that was good enough to deserve this moment, but he was grateful. And was going to make sure she didn't regret whatever made her decide to take this leap. He considered himself savvy at reading people, and he suspected her fast move into intimacy was out of character for her. He didn't want to ponder too much on the why of that.

He just wanted to ponder on…her.

He slid an arm under her legs and along her back, lifting her as he stood. She sighed, her hands clasping his shoulders. He closed the four steps to the bed in record time, lowering her to the mattress without breaking contact. He'd dreamed of having her here, planned, but the rush of excitement at holding her in his arms, in his room, exceeded his imagination.

And his imagination had been mighty damn amazing.

Stretching out over her, he groaned with pleasure at the feeling of her under him. The mattress gave ever so slightly as he did his best to keep his full weight off her while still enjoying the fit and match of their bodies aligning. Of seeing her fiery hair splayed across his pillow. Her emerald green eyes were sultry with want.

She snapped the waistband of his running shorts with a sass that sent a bolt of desire surging through him. He sketched his mouth along her jaw, down her neck to her shoulder and then the soft length of her arm until he could reach her ankle. He inched his fingers under the hem of her dress and bunched the fabric up, up, up her silky leg to her hip.

Arching her back, she bowed upward and stretched her arms overhead in an unmistakable invitation. An invitation he fully intended to accept. He swept her dress up and off...exposing breathtaking curves encased in white lace.

She looked like one of those timeless models painted on the side of an aircraft in the prior century. Pinup luscious and all his for the taking. Or maybe she was taking him, because the way her fingers were caressing his chest, then moved lower still to cradle his erection, had him throbbing to be inside her. Deeply. Fully.

The feel of her hands on him numbed his mind to rational thought. Instincts took over, his whispers of encouragement mixing with her moans as they swept aside the remainder of clothes until—yes—they were skin to skin, heated flesh to flesh. The length of his hard-on pressed on her stomach in a tempting precursor of what it would feel like to have her all around him.

Soon.

Not soon enough, if her eager hands were anything to judge by, as they touched him, explored him...and sheathed him in the condom.

Damn. She was tight... *Tight* or *tense?* Either way, he intended to take care of her.

He slid his hand between them, touching and circling the nub of nerves. Her hips rocked in response, urging him deeper even as he perceived a wince. He didn't consider himself an ego dude about size, but clearly there was an issue here. Possibly she'd been abstinent for a long while? He'd heard of that being an issue for a woman who'd gone for long periods without, but he could also see in her face that talking was going to be a serious mood buster. So he ramped up the foreplay.

And truth be told, taking his time with her was no sacrifice. A bit torturous, but incredibly so.

She grazed her nails down his back to dig into his buttocks. "Why are you waiting? I want this."

He nipped her earlobe and whispered, "And I want this to be good for both of us."

"I know what I'm doing. I'm not naive." She rubbed a knee along his hip.

"I can tell." He smoothed back her hair, smiling. "We're just having some logistic issues here, and taking my time with you is in no way a hardship."

He kissed her neck, devoting his undivided attention to gently licking and tasting along the creamy patch of skin running from her ear to her shoulder. Her pulse picked up speed under his mouth.

Every inch deeper inside her was sweet torture, but he was determined to make sure she didn't regret this. He wanted to be invited back into her bed and he intended to use every touch, taste, instinct in his arsenal to make sure she issued that invitation.

She writhed under him, arching her breasts against his chest. The sensation of her softness against him threatened his tenuous control, but what a sweet temptation. He dipped his head and took a pebbly peak in his mouth, teasing and tugging. And yes, her breathy sigh of approval sent a rush of victory through him. He shifted his attention to the other creamy mound while sliding his hand over the breast he'd abandoned.

Moments melded into each other and he reveled in her relaxing. An interesting dichotomy as her passion rose but her muscles melted. His thrusts slid deeper,

deeper still and he searched her face for the least sign of discomfort and found she was watching him. Which meant she was thinking. He wanted her feeling.

He stilled, angled his mouth over hers and held, then teased the seam of her mouth. She parted quickly, their tongues thrusting, her arms holding tighter to him.

Her knees fell open wider, her feet sliding up higher.

Yes, and in this moment he realized her body was starved for touch. She'd been alone for so long, and he suspected she'd devoted herself totally to her children and not to any kind of social life. With that thought, his hands went into motion. He was bolder, stroking, caressing and massaging along her shoulders, arms, sides, hips, along her thighs. She hugged him closer, tighter, her breathy moans mingling with his groan. Release—his, hers—was so close.

When hers hit, she took him right with her.

Wave after wave of pleasure pounded through his veins.

His arms clasped her closer even as they rolled to their sides, panting. Wordless. Her forehead pressed to his chest.

And words were scarce because while he'd expected sex with Natalie to be amazing, he hadn't expected it to be the best sex ever.

Natalie stretched, luxuriating in this moment. In her choice. He'd brought the dessert to her, along with his sweet tea.

His low-slung running shorts were back on, but his muscles still tempted her. Max's messy hair made him seem somehow even sexier. Plopping down next to her, he traced his fingers along her thigh.

The scents of perspiration and his body wash mingled into a perfume that was just...them.

She was sated. Her body relaxed and her senses hummed. And thank goodness her children slept, the monitor still playing the music softly, no sounds other than an occasional sniffle in their sleep.

She had this pocket of time awhile longer, an incredible, unexpected encounter even though she'd come prepared. She couldn't deny, she was also a little embarrassed at the awkward start as she'd discovered those big hands of his fulfilled every cliché and combined with her abstinence had made for a rather uncomfortable start.

"You're a patient man," she offered, by way of a delicate acknowledgment.

"You're a sensual woman."

Only because he'd made her feel that way. Wow.

"I feel like we should talk about how things started, how I... It had been a long time..."

He pressed a finger to her lips. "I understand. We figured things out, I believe, and when we recover our energy, you'll keep communicating." He kissed her once, twice. "Tell me what you like and don't like, what you want and don't want..."

Her hand behind his neck, she drew him closer. "I want more of you—" she nipped his bottom lip "—and more of the pie."

A moment of the past threatened the present. An image of blond-haired Jeremy entered her mind—their budding relationship. The flowers, the hotel where she'd first slept with her husband. A marriage. A life. Two kids. So much love and it still wasn't enough to keep any of them safe from darkness.

Swallowing, she closed her eyes, willed herself to

stay in this moment. To not slip back to the source of so much pain.

"Yes, ma'am." Laughing, he skimmed his mouth over hers once more before they both dug in to share the rest of the pie and pass the tea back and forth.

Chewing through her last bite, she studied him, wondering…so much. "I don't understand you. Surely there are more experienced, less complicated women out there."

"Less complicated sounds…boring." He leaned forward, resting his chin on his hand.

Swallowing, she tilted her head, trying to understand. "So I'm a challenge to you?"

"Lady, I have challenges in my life all the time and I'm not hopping into bed with them. I just know I want you. And seeing you happy, seeing your face flushed with pleasure, brings me pleasure. That's worth being patient for." His tone was so simple. So measured and assured.

"You and I, together, we don't make sense. Can't you argue with that fact?" And they didn't. Their routines, goals. All those things were worlds apart. And she couldn't take another fissure, another fracture in her life.

There it was again. The past running to overtake her. A flash of her dead husband again. How they stopped talking because it was easier than arguing. That distance made more resonant after his death.

"This last thing I want to do is argue with you. I will say, I can't claim to understand this draw I felt from the moment I clapped eyes on you. But it's real."

Tears gathered in the corners of her eyes, and part of her just wanted to make love again and say to hell with talking, with this sharing that was somehow so much more intimate. But just as she started to lift her hand, something in his eyes gave her pause and bolstered her. Encouraged her to take another chance here.

She breathed. Once. Twice. Willed the tears away. In a small voice, she pressed on. "He was my first love, my first...everything."

He stroked her face with tender fingertips, the rasp of his calluses so gentle. "I'm sorry for your...loss? *Loss* seems like such an inadequate word."

"*Loss...* It's a fair word. One I understand well."

"What do you mean?"

"I was a military wife. I am the mother of a special-needs child. Those two things alone put my marriage under tremendous stress."

A lifetime flashed before her eyes. All the hardships that came with the military life. The disruption of daily life—their routines that had to be started and stopped continuously.

"You and Jeremy had problems?"

"Long deployments. War scars. A child with challenges. Yes, my marriage was going through a rocky patch, and that broke my heart. His, too, I believe. And we both felt helpless to fix things." Natalie released a shuddering breath, the air almost punched free by pain. The aftershocks of his death rocked her still. She knew they always would.

How could they not?

"And then he was deployed again," Max offered, filling in the gaps of the story.

She shook her head, lips thinning to a line. Eyes closed, she willed her tongue to form the words she scarcely uttered. "He volunteered to go."

"He did what?"

"He voluntarily went on this deployment. He said

time apart would be good for us…and now he's…" The word couldn't come out, became lodged in her throat. Threatened her ability to breathe.

"You can't possibly blame yourself."

A bitter laugh accompanied by another wave of threatening tears. She swallowed, finding her voice again. "I understand intellectually, but I'm human. I can't help thinking if he hadn't been trying to put space between us…" She pushed her hair off her forehead. "And then there were the bills from all the specialists for Colby. Deployments come with hazardous-duty pay."

"Sounds like you both had a heavy load on you."

"Sometimes, in my darkest moments, I wonder if he was distracted…or worse, if he put himself in harm's way."

"You think he could have been suicidal?"

She shook her head emphatically. That was a possibility she couldn't bear to entertain and could never know for certain. Still, she found herself whispering words she'd never said to anyone. "I don't think so. But grief is irrational. We weren't communicating. And if in some flash of a moment he thought insurance money would… God, I can't even say it, it hurts too much."

His voice lowered an octave. "I wish there was something I could do to ease this pain you're carrying around."

And just knowing that he wanted to comfort her… that meant so much. A tiny piece of her grief unknotted for a moment.

"Just having you listen helps. There's no one here I feel comfortable telling." She cradled her head between her hands, her voice breaking. This secret—this knowledge—weighed her down every day. She'd had no one to speak to about this. Not her friends. And certainly not her parents, who already blamed her for making poor decisions in regard to her marriage and family.

"I'm glad you feel you can talk to me."

"There's a connection between us." She watched his eyes lift. "I realize that… What? You're surprised I would say that?"

"Yes, I am. I know about this…draw between us, but your standoffish vibes have been strong." He stroked a finger down her cheek. "At least they were until tonight."

"I'm trying to move on. I *want* to move on. But it's easier said than done." She rubbed the spot where her wedding ring had been.

He touched the bare spot. "Seems to me that you are taking steps forward with your life."

"You're just saying that because you have me naked." She tried to lighten the moment, lighten her heart.

"I'm talking about your B and B, the dresses you make, your incredible kids and even that funny, sweet dog you're having trained. From where I'm sitting, you've got life locked and loaded." He leaned forward. "And yes, you're here in bed with me. Beautifully naked."

Her emotions were raw from memories of the past, but those same memories made her all the more certain. She would make the most of this night with Max.

Because life had shown her well that tomorrow was never guaranteed.

The smell of asphalt after the rain entered Max's nostrils. The acidic smell felt like the only constant in his life.

He'd been passed over again by another family.

Fine. He didn't need them.

He didn't need anyone.

Standing beneath the streetlight, he surveyed the city—he had no need to go anywhere, since the group home thought he was at some camping trip. He was good at dodging places that didn't care about having him around anyway.

Out here, crappy as it was, everything and nothing were simultaneously at his fingertips.

The sun sank low on the horizon, setting fire to the skyline. The whole world seemed to be drenched in fire-red hues as a cold wind stung the edges of his exposed cheeks. A hunger rumbled deep in his stomach, and his eyes shifted to the Dumpster behind the Italian restaurant. Every night, they dumped perfectly good bread and pasta.

So what? He wasn't adoptable. Not every kid had the run of the streets like this. The future was as open as this Dumpster. Rules were made for some other people. He'd make his own standards.

Another growl rumbled from his stomach. Light seemed to stream at odd angles from the streetlight as he moved toward the Dumpster.

Flipping open the Dumpster lid, he began digging, looking for a hunk of bread.

Instead, his hands found a soft sheet. The scent of lavender replaced the wet asphalt. Wrapped around him. Felt like home, a concept he hadn't ever really explored...

He flinched, finding himself miles and years away from that Dumpster. The city scene was gone, replaced by a domestic one. Natalie slept next to him, the soft sounds of her breathing grounding him in the present.

She'd shared so much about herself, her past, making herself vulnerable to him. And he couldn't help being moved by that. He couldn't fix her past and her heart, but he could give her ease, pleasure, a moment's forgetfulness.

Watching her sleeping body, he tugged lightly on the edge of the sheet, gathering one deliberate handful at a time toward him and off her. She squeaked once, gripping a fistful, then slowly unfurled her hand and released the crisp white cotton so that... Yes...

He revealed her shoulders, then more as the sheet glided over her breasts, farther, farther...until he unveiled creamy skin with a sprinkling of freckles.

Irresistible.

Angling forward, he pressed his mouth to a smattering of freckles on her hip. She moaned, rolling ever so slightly. He sketched his hand down her leg, sweeping the sheet the rest of the way to the floor. He nuzzled her stomach, feeling the hitch and catch of her breaths, encouraging. Arousing. He kissed his way lower, and lower still until his shoulders nudged apart her legs.

The scent of her was an aphrodisiac he would never forget. Her sensual nature fed his own. Kissing her intimately, he felt a delicate shiver tremble through her whole body. Anchoring her hips in his hands, he tasted her fully, greedy for more but careful not to rush the slow build for her.

She was impossibly sweet and soft. Her fingers skimmed through his hair, a new restlessness in her touch as she arched beneath him.

A flush spread over her skin. A warmth he felt under his palms right before her body quivered.

She writhed and shuddered with her release. Her head pushed back into the pillow and she pressed her wrist over her mouth to hold in her gasps and moans of pleasure. He burned to take her somewhere private, where she could revel in her release with full abandon.

And he would, he vowed. He would find a way to have her all to himself. Soon.

Seven

After stacking the orange pottery plates together, Natalie made her way to the sink, careful not to spill any of the toast crumbs on the floor. Her children had just left for preschool and the guests were already all checked out, leaving her in relative silence.

Peace seemed so rare these days.

She turned on the water, letting it heat up as she put the plates in the deep sink. Pumping soap onto the sponge, she thought back to the taste of Max—the night they'd shared together.

For a moment, she imagined his hands around her, craved that touch. Being close to him had been surprising in more ways than she could have expected. The connection she felt to him was more combustible than she would have predicted. She'd been looking for more of a simple release, a way to deal with this crazy obsession.

But his touch had been...electric. Surprisingly tender. Beautifully intuitive.

The night would have been perfect, if only her body hadn't carried a betrayal. She'd expected a bit of adjustment after so long without sex. She had not expected quite so much, from the combination of abstinence and his size. His skill as a lover had brought her to completion, but her body was definitely tender. She almost felt as if she was revisiting the morning after losing her virginity.

And that frustrated her. She wanted to just lose herself in a wild, simple, brief affair. Something that wasn't going to happen until she figured out this issue with her body.

As she scrubbed the plates, the sound of heavy footfalls sounded behind her, cutting short her thoughts. Glancing over her shoulder, she saw Max approach. Stomach fluttering, she turned back to her work.

Max slipped behind her, his arms drawing her to him. Hot breath curled around the nape of her neck. He kissed tender skin there, reminding her of all the ways she'd come undone in his arms the night before. His intense attention to detail, always apparent in his job, had been a delicious gift in bed. Just thinking about that made her breath quicken, and she melted into that moment.

But something else worked its way into those sensual thoughts. Though the guests had all checked out for the day, there was still a chance that she and Max could be spotted.

Swallowing, she spun around, grabbing a dish towel before she placed her hands on his muscled chest. "We need to talk."

She took a deep breath, willing her pulse to slow down. Her brain to catch up with her senses.

He squinted, as if trying to analyze her words like

computer code. She could see his detective gears spinning. "That sounds ominous," he said.

"It's not..." Her shoulders sagged a bit, and she seemed to shrink away from him.

"About what?"

A long sigh gave her enough time to gather her thoughts. And courage. "About how we're going to handle things now that we're sleeping together and living under the same roof."

He reached out to touch her arm. Careful. Enough to send a shiver down her spine. "To be clear, we're not living under the same roof. It's your roof. I'm a guest, a boarder. I understand that. So, if you were panicking that I expect to move into your bedroom, then put your mind at rest."

She'd never even considered the possibility. The idea of nightly access to Max was enough to send her imagination into overdrive. But, of course, that wasn't happening. "Okay, I'm glad you realize that. But that wasn't what I was going to say." A sad kind of smile tugged at her heart as well as her mouth as she stared at him. Took in his dark features and the concern that splintered across his eyes.

"Well, hell. You sure put me in my place."

"I apologize. It's not my way to make someone uncomfortable. But I do have to say, you don't look particularly wounded."

An uncomfortable laugh escaped his lips. Raising his eyebrow, he gestured. "Say your piece, woman."

"I need for you to be careful outside the bedroom."

"Clarify that?"

"I don't want gossip among the guests. I have a professional reputation to maintain. We may have gone on a date, but I have to live in this town afterward." That was the reality. Whatever existed between her and Max was temporary. He would leave because, as he pointed out, he was a boarder. This transient relationship could not impact her standing in this town.

"After I leave, you mean," he said, eyes burning into hers.

She raised her chin, leveling him with a stare all her own. "Yes, that's exactly what I mean."

"You're writing me off awfully fast."

She chewed her lip, pulling away from him. Needing to remember to build space between them and guard her heart. "You know you're going home, more likely sooner rather than later."

"Still, gone isn't exactly...gone." He wiggled his hand around above his head. "I have an airplane. I could be here more often than planned."

"That's all hypothetical. I'm talking about today. About this town...about my children."

"Even if I were to stay somewhere else, they already know me separate from you. I—and others—enjoy being part of their lives. It's about more than helping you. They're good kids who've been through a lot."

"I realize that. And I believe the more people who contribute positive moments to their lives, the better. Truly. I'm grateful for the way people rally around them." She leaned back against the counter, her T-shirt brushing against water, dampening her back.

"They're great kids. You're a great person."

"Thank you. Just... Let's not be a couple around them." She couldn't enter this casually for the sake of her children. Bringing a man into their lives was a big deal. Natalie needed whoever that man was to be a stable force.

He nodded, understanding the implications of her

statement. "It's not about gossip. It's about your children hearing gossip and making assumptions."

"They may not really remember Jeremy, but they know they lost their dad. They know other children have fathers. They feel the loss and I can't have them creating false expectations because you're nice and you're here and they assume we're a couple."

He took his own step back now, vision seeming to travel back, away from the moment. Max took a measured breath before answering. "I understand what it feels like to be a child wanting a father, then wanting any family at all. I would never put any child through the pain of having those hopes dashed."

The ache in her stomach screamed. Heat flooded her cheeks and she reached out for him, seeking his hand. Needing to connect. "Max, I'm sorry. I should have thought that and realized you would understand. I—"

"You have nothing to apologize for. You're looking out for your kids. That makes you a good mother, and quite frankly, it makes me like you all the more."

"You like me?" She couldn't resist the urge to flirt, just a little.

"Yes, I do like you. You're an incredibly likable woman." He leaned in and whispered, "And I really like you with your clothes off."

"Well, the guests have checked out and no one's due in. The kids are at preschool…" Temptation pulled at her. She felt the connection in the air between them.

"Hmm… I would take that as an invitation, but then I know this place well. There's always traffic."

"I do have a dress client coming by in a half hour."

A devilish grin spread across his face as he squeezed her hand. "Then how about we make out in the pantry?"

With ease, he lifted her off her feet and brought them to the kitchen pantry—away from any and all prying eyes.

The last two days had unfolded at a breakneck speed of work for him and an uptick in business for Natalie, as well. Max attributed that to the lack of time together, the distance.

Or rather he could have.

But her standoffish vibe was clear, granted it was in an understated way. She was never rude to anyone. But there was no mistaking that some of her busyness was self-inflicted.

Morning sun streamed through the front windows of the sitting area, and Max pored over documents in the common area of the B and B, enjoying the generous amount of natural light the two huge windows provided. He thumbed through a St. Cloud Security Solutions company report on an overseas project. His business partner and the company's chief technology officer, Will Brady, had been keeping him up-to-date on details from the main office. Balancing all his contacts and projects the last few days had drained him. Keeping up with business back in Seattle and working late here when people were most often free for interviews was more challenging than he anticipated.

That didn't leave him much time to spend with Natalie, especially given how early she woke to prepare breakfast for her customers. His and Natalie's paths weren't crossing much privately—only a few stolen kisses that she clearly enjoyed, but there hadn't been a chance for anything more. And certainly not an opportunity for any lengthy discussion. Was that deliberate on her part or accidental?

Stealing a glance across the room, he watched Miss Molly curl around Colby's feet. The dog let out an audible sigh, her soulful brown eyes shifting around the room, head tilting to look at Margie and Lexie.

Natalie's words echoed in his mind, along with her step back when it came to going to bed together again. He didn't so much sense a no, but more of a "not right now." Maybe she was figuring things out in her mind in regard to her children. He respected what she'd said. Her children had been through a lot very young. His life on the streets had made him even more empathetic to struggles. And he wasn't going to be here long... something that should be a relief, since no one could get overly attached to him.

Right? The thought didn't bring him as much comfort as it should have.

Lexie stood up, tapped Margie on the shoulder. She cupped her hands together and leaned on the woman's lap, whispering in her ear. Margie's face softened and she nodded.

"Yes, you can go see your mom, sweetie." Margie gave her a hug, eliciting a squeal of delight from Lexie. She scampered away, disappearing from view.

Margie handed crayons to Colby, and he began to color another fish. Colby's fish drawings were all around the house, hanging on the fridge, in the common room. He was actually quite good, his details precise with scales and gills.

The little boy popped a Goldfish cracker into his mouth and chewed thoughtfully. Max wondered what it was about the water that intrigued Colby. Even his room was sea themed.

Closing his laptop and shoving his documents into a manila file folder, Max followed what his gut instincts were telling him. He walked over to the corner table with his hands in his pockets and cleared his throat. "Margie, if you want to take a break, I can hang out with Colby."

The older woman glanced up, smiling. "Well, if you're sure you don't mind, I would like to stretch my legs and refill my glass of tea."

"Take your time. I'll send a shout-out if I get in over my head," Max said and nodded. Then he shifted his attention to the four-year-old, who carefully picked up a pretzel stick, dipped it in peanut butter, then dabbed a small fish cracker with the sticky end.

Ingenious.

But then he'd seen dozens of ways Natalie multi-tasked as a mother while managing her B and B and wedding-dress-design business. That humbled him more than a little as he considered he had only himself and his company to think about. Hell, some days he barely had time left over to eat away from the computer.

He glanced at Colby again, the boy so silent, such a mystery to Max still. The child pretty much only let Miss Molly near him for any extended length of time. The golden retriever's tail thumped on the floor as she leaned against Colby's legs.

Maybe there was a way to accomplish a few goals at once. Give Natalie a break. Show her he knew how to let the kids have fun without them growing too attached. And yes, give Colby a nice outing, one of the child's choosing. "Do you want to go fishing?"

Colby chewed thoughtfully, then set aside his peanut butter–covered pretzel stick. "Gotta ask my mom."

"Of course." He should have thought to reassure the boy of that right away, but he hadn't spent much time with kids since leaving foster care. "But if you don't want to go, then there's no need to even ask her."

"I don't understand."

"I want to know that it's something you would enjoy."

Colby nodded. "Fishing is quiet. I like quiet."

"Good. I like quiet, too." There weren't many silent moments in crowded group homes and overcrowded foster families. But Max had had one foster father who'd always woken up earlier than the others to cook breakfast and he'd let Max join him. They hadn't spoken much, but Max had learned more, gained more confidence, in those near-silent exchanges than during any other time growing up.

"I don't like taking it off the hook. It feels weird."

"I can handle that part. Are you okay with eating the fish?"

Colby grinned and held up his cup of crackers, rattling them. "I like all kinds of fish. But I mostly like the real kind grilled. And corn on the cob, too."

And right there, the boy had said the most words at once in Max's presence.

The sense of victory rivaled winning a multimillion-dollar contract. The feeling gave him a moment's pause. This simple outing was supposed to be about Colby... not about Max. He was supposed to be careful the kid didn't grow too attached to him.

Max hadn't considered he might actually become attached to the child.

Clearing his throat and shaking off the unsettling feeling, Max stood, careful not to move in too close to the boy and encroach on his personal space. "Let's talk to your mom."

They made their way to the sewing room. Glancing around, he realized how busy she was with the client. An explosion of lace and patterns seemed to occupy every spare surface. Chaos contained, but only barely.

Somehow amid all this chaos, Lexie managed to find sleep. She was curled up on the nap mat and did not stir.

He waited for a break in her conversation with the customer, then asked softly, "Natalie, do you mind if Colby goes fishing with me?"

She glanced at him, then at the customer and over at napping Lexie. He could see her independence at war with her need for help. "Max, are you sure you don't mind?"

"I wouldn't have offered if I didn't mean it."

Colby stepped inside the room, shuffling his feet, eyes darting. "Please, Mom."

Her face melted into a smile. "Of course, son. But you have to promise me you'll listen to Mr. Max and don't wander off. Okay? Promise?"

Colby nodded solemnly. "Promise."

Her smile growing, she gazed at Max. "Thank you so much for the generous offer. There's fishing gear in the shed out back. And please be sure to use the extra car seat in the mudroom."

Max nodded, already planning a quick trip to the store because he wasn't using her dead husband's gear. "We'll do our best to bring home food for all."

He drove them to the local fishing store for an array of supplies. Colby picked out two poles and Max chose one. They loaded up his SUV with tackle and bait. Colby seemed excited by the lures, and his smile grew as they approached a nearby river.

An hour had passed by in a whir of activity. They'd managed to catch three sizable fish. Colby clapped after he brought the first fish to shore, excitement wriggling through his little body. Three fish were chilling in the icebox they'd brought, certainly enough for dinner.

The silence of the last twenty minutes felt soothing.

Max felt himself decompress as they sat side by side, listening to the softer sounds of the river as it whirred by. He'd purposely chosen a spot away from some local picnickers, and enjoyed the view of the houses on the other side of the water and the big live oaks shading a bend in the river. Every now and then, a fish jumped, the splash making a wet plunk. Other than that, the day was quiet. The silence had attracted him to computer work. He liked the self-reliance that silence forced.

Colby seemed to enjoy the quiet, as well.

To make the boy feel as comfortable as possible, they'd brought Miss Molly. Max had been concerned the dog might bark and scare way the fish, but the golden retriever was as quiet as a church mouse. She simply rested her head on Colby's leg, her wide brown eyes watchful, alert, but calm. Max was starting to buy into this whole service-dog angle for autism. It had seemed kinda fuzzy wuzzy before. Not very scientific. But Max had been watching. And the dog employed techniques to keep Colby calm that went beyond the boy just feeling comfortable with his four-legged companion. Pressure at just the right moment to stop a meltdown. Alerting Natalie when Colby was growing agitated. The list went on and every time Margie came by for lessons, they fine-tuned training, increment by increment.

Colby cast a quick glance Max's way, then turned his face back to the water. "My dad isn't coming home."

The air whooshed from Max's lungs. This conversation had gone deeper than he'd expected. Deeper than he thought Natalie would want. But right now Max had to handle this as best he could for Colby's sake. "I'm very sorry about that."

He nodded, his head moving like the jerky fishing bobber. "Mom's sad."

Of course she was. Could that be a part of her pulling away? And how damn wrong was it to feel jealous of a dead man? "And what about you?"

"Lexie's sad."

"And you?" Max asked again.

The grief in the boy's normally rather flat tones tore at Max. "I don't like when people are sad."

"I don't either, buddy."

"I'm not your buddy."

"Why do you say that?"

"You don't know me."

"All right. Fair enough." More silence sprang up, allowing Max to contemplate the boy's words. Max knew what it was like to be wary of trusting other adults—part of why he'd been so drawn to the logic of computers. An idea tugged at him. He cranked his reel in, then cast again. "Colby, when we finish up here, would you like me to show you some fishing games on my computer?"

"Yes, please." He nodded eagerly, still keeping his face forward. "But we're still gonna grill our fish, right?"

"Absolutely," Max said without hesitation, pumped at the boy's enthusiasm over the computer idea. "Absolutely."

And he was unsettled at how much this victory meant to him.

The sun had already receded from the horizon as Natalie stood at the sink and cleared off the supper dishes. She'd tucked her children into bed, and sleep had found them quickly.

Colby had gone to sleep so quickly and deeply he hadn't even needed his weighted blanket that helped him with sensory issues. He'd clearly enjoyed his afternoon with Max. Which, of course, made her happy.

But, God, it worried her a little, too. She hated that she had to worry about that, since she wanted desperately to see more signs of him connecting with people.

"You're quite the chef." She scraped the traces of grilled catfish, corn on the cob and a raisin-and-rice salad into the garbage disposal.

"You should see me in my own domain." He sprayed cleaning solution on the kitchen table. The gesture didn't go unnoticed by her. Receiving help wasn't something she was accustomed to, and she appreciated it.

Moving from the trash can to the sink, she pressed on. "Your house in Seattle?"

"Condo actually, in my company's St. Cloud Tower. It keeps me close to work."

"A condo. In Seattle." She couldn't imagine living without a yard for her children and Miss Molly to run in.

"I haven't had much use for a yard with all the time I spend away from home. But I can see the benefits of a porch swing." He winked. "I'll have to look into installing one on my rooftop garden."

For a moment, her mind wandered to the rooftop garden. What it would be like to nestle next to him in the cold Seattle air on that yet-to-be-installed porch swing. "I imagine that would be a lovely view."

"You should come see it."

She just laughed softly. Like that was even possible.

"You should," he said with unmistakable sincerity. "I could cook for you there. My kitchen is a sight to behold."

"Unlike here?" She waved around her kitchen. Homey, sure. Up to code. Clean. But a long way from the high-tech sort of place a billionaire could afford.

"That's not what I meant. It's up to the chef to create. I was simply stating what I could do, and what I would like to do for you." He moved toward her and kissed the nape of her neck.

Her throat bobbed as she swallowed, breathing in his scent. Musky temptation. But she had her reservations…like how to figure out a way to make things more comfortable between them. Hell, how to even tell him. "You have already done so much—cooking me dinner, fixing my sink and all you're doing for the town."

He ran soft fingers up and down her arm, sending shivers through her body. "We're talking about you and me."

"This is strange territory for me, this whole dating world. It's been so long I've forgotten the rules." Her fingers found his.

He lifted her hand to his lips. Kissed her, maintaining eye contact. "There are no rules. Only what you and I want."

"If only it could be that simple." She sighed, avoiding his gaze, along with telling him her thoughts. Aside from her being embarrassed, men could be so…sensitive, when it came to how things went in the bedroom. Her hair obscured her vision.

"It can be."

"How?"

"I pour a glass of wine for you and grab a beer for myself and we go outside, sit on your porch swing. We can talk, look at the stars, make out a little."

"What if I want more?" At some point. Because she really did.

"Oh, we're going to have more. But I can sense from you that tonight is not the right time for that."

"Seriously?"

"Yes." He touched her hair. "You still have things going on in your mind, and there's the issue with not wanting gossip."

She swallowed hard to give herself time to weigh her words. To be sure of what she wanted to say. "I guess it's unrealistic for me to think the town expects me to never see anyone. And you did an admirable job with Colby today." She felt like she was standing on the edge of something...important. "So as long as I'm not making a spectacle of myself and you can handle that I need a couple of steps back to regroup...?"

Natalie left the thought unfinished rather than continue her nervous ramble.

He stepped close to her, closer still until their bodies brushed if not their lips. "Lady, I hear what you are saying and want to reassure you. I am in control of myself. You could take off all your clothes here, now, and nothing would happen tonight. I want everything to be right for you."

At the sound of his syllables, a rush went through her. Her heart beat out of time as she considered his control.

And she found she did trust him at his word. As much as she would enjoy being intimate with him again, this was all moving so quickly between them, at warp speed, actually. And an old-fashioned evening date in her backyard could give her the info she needed to help protect her heart.

Or would it sink her deeper into temptation's way?

Eight

As Max approached Natalie, who was sitting on the porch swing, his breath hitched. The night was perfect in a way he could barely quantify. The whole vibe, the moment, was just right there in the pocket with a rightness he couldn't deny. From the woman in front of him, to this idyllic haven she'd created on her property.

The hooting of an owl mixed with the gentle creak of the porch swing. He extended the glass of chardonnay to her, his fingers grazing hers.

That awareness returned to his limbs, his chest. Damn. Her emerald eyes were grateful as she took a sip of the wine.

Sitting next to her, he stretched his arm around her back. Natalie settled into him, that limber body pressed up against his chest.

It was a perfect contrast of warmth to the increasingly cool September air. The B and B had dull lights at best, providing a somewhat uninterrupted view of the stars in the sky.

Taking a swig of his beer, he embraced everything—the sounds, the air, the potential of the ridiculously sexy woman next to him. Her soft curls cast shadows across her face in the shuttered porch light, making her look alluring. Mysterious. Sexy as hell.

Next to him, Natalie sighed deeply, swaying more into the rhythm of the swing. Tempting him and testing his resolve.

He'd meant his vow not to take her to bed tonight. He was a man of patience and she clearly needed space to process what had happened between them.

And he had to admit, their night together had moved him more than he'd expected.

She was right. They were moving fast—both of them.

No question, he wanted to be with her again, and he wasn't sure where this crazy draw was headed. He didn't know where it could go. He couldn't ignore the importance of being careful for her kids. Great kids who were fast becoming more than just Natalie's children.

They were people in their own right.

Lexie.

Colby.

The dinner tonight had tasted better than any in recent memory and he had to be honest with himself. It was the company that added the special seasoning that flavored the meal to perfection.

So where did that leave him? He understood her concerns and reservations. Maybe it was time to help her understand more about what made him the man he'd become. A man who wasn't right for her but wanted her all the same. A man who wasn't good at denying himself what he wanted except he had to be that man. For her, tonight at least.

But tomorrow? Away from here and prying eyes?

He rested his beer on his knee and tucked her to his side. "I know how to cook because of this one foster home I lived in. It was a really good home. People talk about the bad ones so much, and sure, there are some." He shook his head. "But there are some good and amazing people out there opening their homes to children in need. Not enough of them. But plenty."

"And you learned to cook in one of those homes because of the foster mom?"

Memories flashed before his mind's eye. A montage of baking in the well-lit kitchen. Lessons in cooking fettuccine alfredo, lasagna, chimichangas and frittata. Eliot, his foster dad, arranging all the supplies on a faded laminate countertop. "Because of the foster dad. He did all the cooking and made a point of teaching us kids. He told us his wife worked hard and this was his way of pulling his weight. He also told us we would likely live on our own at some point in our lives and that the best way to save money was to cook for ourselves. Eating out was a treat, but not always the financially wisest or the healthiest move."

"Valid points and smart of him to teach you kids that." Her voice was soft and soothing, stroking along the edges of those memories.

"He was a wise man. I learned a lot from him." And back then he'd been hungry to learn and daring to hope he might, just might, get to stick around there long enough to learn a lot.

"Like what?"

A hefty sigh damn near deflated him. Of all the foster homes, that one with Eliot had been the closest he'd ever gotten to having a family. The memory of what-if still pained him. "How to change a tire. How to use crap to make things, which ultimately led me to build my first computer by Dumpster diving behind a few business offices and a computer store."

"How old were you while you were there?"

"For a little over a year when I was thirteen." He'd learned a lot in that year, things that had stuck with him long after he left. He'd just been too mad then to realize it.

"What happened?"

A knot formed in his chest. "He had a stroke, a really bad one. His wife couldn't take care of him and all of us foster kids. She wanted to." He believed that now, even though then he'd been so angry he'd doubted her. "But the system thought otherwise about her ability to jug-gle his care with raising fosters and they moved us all."

"I'm so sorry." She clasped his hand and rubbed lightly.

"That's life. It's not always fair and a person has to accept the things beyond control—or go crazy." He shrugged, swirling the beer in his bottle.

"You figured that out at thirteen?"

"Hell, no. My foster dad told me that, slowly, with drool pooling in one corner of his mouth, his left side almost totally paralyzed from the stroke. I just didn't fully accept it until later."

She angled her face to see him, her eyes searching his. "How is he doing now?"

"He died when I was nineteen." He tore his gaze away from hers and tipped up his beer for a long swig. "But I think of him when I cook and I feel like I'm hon-oring his memory. The way I see it, the foster system isn't perfect, but I made it through. I can focus on the good, and do what I can to help fix the broken."

"Fix the broken?" she asked sympathetically, lifting her wineglass to her lips. "How do you do that?"

"Ah, that's a story for another day."

Her eyes went wide and she lowered her glass. "You're a secret philanthropist."

He laughed lightly and tugged a lock of her red hair—God, it was silky. "If I talk about it, then it's not a secret, is it?"

"Magazines call you a billionaire playboy, but then go around doing all these nice things for people."

He shifted in the seat, uncomfortable with the turn of the conversation. "Don't romanticize me, Natalie. I've lived a footloose life as an adult, living my way. It's easy to be nice with all this money and freedom at my disposal."

"Max, you're trying to paint such a bad boy—"

He kissed her. Held her lips with his, not pulling away for even a second as he set aside his beer bottle, then filched her crystal glass to put it down. Hands free now, he wrapped his arms around her and hauled her close, giving his all to kissing her. The taste of wine on her tongue was almost as intoxicating as the woman herself.

And yes, having her in his arms was better than being tempted to talk more. She had a way of drawing things from him he hadn't thought about in years, and wasn't sure he wanted to think about now.

Losing himself in her was far preferable to visiting the past. And damn, he would like to completely lose himself in her body.

And Natalie swayed closer to him, her breasts flat against his chest, her fingers thrusting up and into his hair. She breathed a husky moan against his mouth. "I thought you said you're okay with my need for a bit of breathing room. That we weren't going to sleep together tonight."

"We aren't." He grinned, enjoying the sound of temptation in her voice. He could have her, but he could still sense the reservation in her. She might have come to his room, but clearly something about that gave her pause and she had the right to say no. And he would respect that, even as he gently pursued her. He wasn't going to risk spooking her altogether. "But I never said I wasn't going to kiss you absolutely senseless. Which now that I have done, I will say—" he kissed her lips, then the tip of her nose "—good night."

Training days in the yard with Margie always gave Natalie hope.

Hope for a fuller life for her son. Hope that somehow she was managing to give her children what they needed to grow into productive, happy adults. Listening to Max talk about his childhood reminded her of the lifetime of emotional scars that could be left on a person from their youth.

Hearing her son and daughter laugh was the sweetest reassurance of all. Today, Margie had been playing hide-and-seek with the kids and the dog, what she termed one of the early foundations of teaching K-9 search-and-rescue. While Miss Molly wouldn't be taking that path with her working life, she could be called upon to find Colby if he wandered off—not an unheard of occurrence for her brilliant, reticent son.

Lexie and Colby had spent the past hour hiding in different places around the yard, giving Miss Molly variations of clues to find them—anything from whispering, to squeaking a toy, even wearing a shirt from the dirty laundry pile to give Miss Molly an extra whiff of their scent on the breeze.

Miss Molly was a natural.

Natalie leaned against a tree, taking in the sight of Miss Molly tunneling under an upside-down kiddie pool, where her children were curled up together, giggling.

Lexie wrapped her arms around Miss Molly's neck and hugged gently. "Love you, my puppy." She glanced up at Margie. "This is fun. I like this game."

Margie adjusted the treat pouch strapped around her waist. "I'm happy to hear that. We'll play that some more in the future, all right?"

"Yes, yes, yes, yes!" Lexie wriggled farther out from under the baby pool.

"Yeah," Colby said simply, but his enthusiasm showed in how he leaped to his feet, upending the plastic pool.

Natalie pushed herself away from the tree and knelt by her children. "Margie's going to work on leash walking now, so would the two of you play in the sandbox? I'll be right here in eyesight and you can call me if you need me."

"Okeydoke." Lexie hugged her mom hard and pressed a sticky kiss on Natalie's cheek.

Colby nodded, following his sister to the wooden sandbox full of shovels and buckets and toy trucks.

"Miss Molly, come." Margie issued the command low and firm, her alpha-style authority a fun contradiction coming from the slight, wiry woman. Miss Molly stopped dead in her tracks, pivoted on her paws and trotted back toward them.

Even after these months of training since Natalie had

adopted Miss Molly from the Royal Safe Haven Animal Shelter and started the golden retriever's training, Natalie still found Margie's ability to command the dog with such ease impressive. That was why she was the professional, after all.

Miss Molly still had a lot of training to accomplish, but Margie assured them all was on track. Kneeling, the trainer hooked a service-dog-in-training vest on the yellow dog.

Glancing to the left, Natalie checked on her kids in the sandbox. Lexie and Colby had constructed a rather lopsided sand castle. Her daughter's infectious laughter mingled with the sounds of birdcalls and the hum of conversations on the front porch. Even Colby seemed relaxed today. Her heart squeezed, returning her attention back to Margie and training. Natalie hoped that Miss Molly's training would give her son every advantage in the world.

As Margie passed over a treat from her pouch, Natalie took a deep breath. The scent of fallen leaves filled her. She loved this time of year.

Her mind wandered a bit, picking up a well-worn trail in which she stored the recent memories of Max. His confident grin and mischievous eyes. The way his kisses hinted at his duality. Every kiss with him fused strength to passion, abandon to control. An addictive combination, if she were being truthful.

Last night had been a bit more of a high-stakes moment. The evening had unfolded with perfect ease. A combination of everything she needed. His kiss, his measured ability to keep things from escalating too far. Respecting her wishes and boundaries.

He'd been great with her kids. Especially Colby. He seemed to understand how to engage with him. Max was different than a lot of her friends in town, who, at first, tried to smother Colby with well-meaning affection. It had taken her closest friends some time to understand physical touch had to be dictated by Colby. But Max fell into a pattern with Colby. For that she was grateful.

He'd even shared more about his life last night, become more real by the hour. Her mind again returned to the kiss at the end of the night.

She'd wanted to go further...but there was still an awkwardness she couldn't get past.

Giving Miss Molly a hand and spoken command—*let's go*—Margie started a brisk walk toward the gate, Natalie walking alongside. They would walk the yard, and the perimeter, the children always in sight, while still working the training.

Margie made Miss Molly wait at the gate, then proceed forward on command. A few steps later, the trainer glanced at Natalie. "Honey, what's wrong?"

"I'm fine, really," Natalie said quickly. Too eager. The words betrayed her.

"You're actually a really a bad liar." Margie's eyebrows shot heavenward.

"Look around you. My life is complicated. I'm exhausted and sad and overworked. That's all." Natalie walked toward the cars. The dog seemed to be getting the message that when she wore her vest during an outing, she wasn't allowed to sniff. This had proven to be the hardest part of working with Miss Molly, but they were making progress.

"You've been that before and something's different. I want to help if I can. If you want me to. Does it have something to do with that hot, young boarder of yours?" Margie walked alongside Miss Molly, her eyes on the dog's movements but she was still concentrating on the conversation. "If he's messing with your heart, there are people in this town who will knock him down a peg or two."

"He's not playing with my heart at all. He's been completely forthright. I've been upfront with him, as well…"

"Then…?"

"It's too embarrassing to say." Natalie lowered her voice, eying her neighbors pushing their toddler on a swing hanging from a fat oak branch. Her heart squeezed with the beauty of all that promise.

Margie ducked her head conspirator-style. "Then I'm guessing it's about sex?"

And there it was. She'd slept with Max. He'd made sure she was satisfied. She wanted to go to bed with him again—needed a passionate affair. Her body was on fire every time he came near. Still… "How crazy is that? I've been married, but…" She shook her head. "It's kind of embarrassing."

"Can you talk to your mother?"

"Heavens, no." Natalie shuddered at the thought. What a way to make things more embarrassing. At best she would get either a lecture or encouragement to pursue Max because of his wealth.

"Well, honey, you clearly need to speak with someone. We girls have to stick together and talk. Too much is kept secret out of embarrassment, and that makes me sad."

Natalie lengthened her stride to keep up, each breath shaking free thoughts through her mind like the rustling trees shedding leaves. "I want to be with him, I want an affair. I need an affair, something just for me."

"What's stopping you?"

"My husband was my first, my only, and, um, there's a size difference. Max was patient...and wonderful, but still, things were uncomfortable."

"Oh, my. That puts a damper on a moment, doesn't it? Could also be your extended period of abstinence making the situation even more complicated?"

"I considered that."

"These things happen. Happened to me when I went through menopause and my body went into seventy kinds of crazy changes. I learned from my sister that it can happen to cancer patients after treatments or surgery."

"That's so sad. How did I not know that?"

"We women need to talk more. It's silly to be embarrassed about our bodies and finding what feels good."

No one had ever been so candid with her. Not even her friends in college had talked about these matters so openly. A blush heated her skin. She couldn't control it, and it deepened into what felt like a bad sunburn.

"See, why are you blushing? Your man was gone a lot. My Terence was a traveling salesman. The week on the road could be long. I invested in some toys and the separation was less stressful."

"I really can't believe we're having this conversation."

"Fair enough. Boundaries should be respected. How about this? Do some reading online. There's a wealth of information on all the subjects I mention and ways to help ease that discomfort. You deserve to enjoy yourself and enjoy that hot, young man of yours."

Could it be that simple? Some practical answers to helping her body along and then going for what she wanted?

Take something for herself?

Take Max.

Damn, that had such an exciting sound she couldn't imagine saying no. If only life wasn't so complicated by her history with her dead husband, by being a single mother with children who deserved to be her priority.

And still, she couldn't deny, against her better judgment, she wanted Max.

Eyes growing heavy, Max forced himself to concentrate on the content on his tablet. As he sat on his bed against the overstuffed pillows, sleep tugged at him.

Stretching out, he readjusted. Propped his head in his hand. He needed to learn just a little bit more.

Max had never backed down from a challenge yet. After today, he wanted to ensure that he could be more helpful to Natalie. Which was why he'd spent the last two hours reading articles about dog training.

Max was a self-taught hacker—it had launched his cybercareer. He possessed a confidence that, given enough reading and research, he could figure anything out. It was a useful trait in his line of work. It probably was why he was so successful at his job. His need to know and understand things drove him to keep pressing on in spite of hitting brick wall after brick wall in investigating this maverick cybercreep.

A knock reinvigorated him, causing him to snap his attention from screen to door.

"Come in." As the words left his mouth, he hoped it was Natalie.

Sure enough, as if some magic prayer had been answered, she appeared at the threshold.

Damn.

Her damp hair fell in waves, adding to the feminine softness in her features. As she held up the phone that allowed her to listen to her children, her green eyes were filled with hope. And something else. Something he was sure was also present in his hungry gaze.

A faint smile played on her lips as she pulled innocently on her loose yellow sundress. Stepping all the way into his room, she shut the door behind her. Took a deep sigh and stared at him.

He took in the sight of her. From the damp hair and bare feet, it was clear she had just showered. She had come to him renewed, that electricity stronger than ever before.

She shut the door and leaned back against it. "I've been doing some reading myself."

Where was she going with this? "Reading is good."

"Informational reading," she said with extra emphasis, biting her bottom lip.

"Okay." What was he missing?

"On our issue."

"What issue might that be?" He placed his tablet on the bedside table and sat on the edge of the mattress.

"This is embarrassing to say—" she scrunched her nose and braced her shoulders, creamy shoulders bare with just the straps of her sundress "—so I'm going to spill it all really quickly and I need you not to interrupt so I can just get it out there. All right?"

He nodded, staying silent, curious as hell as to what she was going to reveal. She looked so serious and intense.

And nervous.

The last thing he wanted was for her to feel apprehensive around him.

"Clearly you had to have noticed that when we had sex, there was some discomfort. We talked about abstinence being an issue. You're also, um, I don't want to sound disloyal, but there's a size issue, too."

Size? His brain went on stun for a moment, not sure he'd heard her correctly; then he thought back to their night together, needing to go slow, to give her time to adjust and realized, holy hell, she'd been more than a little uncomfortable.

He wanted to launch from the bed and close the space between them, cradle her close and make sure she was okay, but she had a distinct stay-back expression, her eyes filled with the unmistakable need to say more.

But he had something to say first. "Natalie, if I hurt you, then, God, I'm so sorry—"

She held up a hand. "No, you didn't hurt me and you have nothing to apologize for. You're…more. So I read up on how to help make things easier for us and I have ideas. Why are you smiling? I'm being serious here."

Was he grinning? Hell, yes. "You want to have sex with me again. Of course I'm smiling." And he was doing his best not to just jump her, because she was here and he was throbbing to have her under him.

Over him.

Beside him.

"I'm trying to be serious here."

"Okay, I can be very serious about having sex with you. Tell me more about your research."

"You don't look very serious."

"Oh, I can assure you." He stood and moved toward her. "When it comes to making sure you are thoroughly, completely, blissfully satisfied, you have my one hundred percent undivided, serious attention."

Her eyes flicked to his as he closed the distance between them. Her eyebrows rose, anticipation showing on her face. Inviting.

Max's hands went into her hair, and he let a soft triumphant laugh roll free as he brought his face to hers. He could feel the smile in her cheeks.

They stayed at the precipice of a kiss for a moment, sharing breaths. Natalie's hands wrapped around him, tightly, urgently.

Kissing her caused his whole body to pulse with life. Quickly. Fully. Because, there was no denying the truth. A kiss from Natalie topped anything he'd felt with women in the past.

Right now he couldn't even bring their names or faces to mind.

His thoughts, his gaze, even his breath, were all focused on *Natalie*.

Nine

Max's skilled tongue and roving fingers had Natalie's toes curling. With a heavy inhale, she soaked in his hot breath on her skin, the subtle nudges pushing her closer. And closer.

They'd barely begun, and this man had somehow already had her pushing on the throes of total passion.

"Hold right there." His deep voice rumbled in her ear.

Her eyes fluttered open as she stared at him in amazement. Her body was still ablaze from his touch. "Excuse me?"

"Don't move." He sprang to his feet, crossed to the oak dresser and opened the top drawer. "Close your eyes."

"Um, I'm not so sure about that." Angling her head to the side, she studied him in the dull yellow light of the room. God, he was so starkly handsome. "That requires a lot of trust."

"You're here, so I hope that means you trust me." He

winked. "If that's the case, I promise to do my best to make sure you won't be disappointed." He tapped her eyebrows one after the other, encouraging her.

"Okay, then." She shut her eyes tight, resisting the urge to peek, though curiosity gnawed at her. Nerves pulled at her, along with anticipation. She wanted this. She was determined this time she could lose herself without reservation. She'd done her best to prepare, to absolutely make the most of this moment.

Which would be helped tremendously by taking control of her nerves.

One deep breath at a time, she pushed away concerns and sank into the present. Only here. Only now.

Natalie began to enjoy a sensation of sounds. She could hear his muffled footsteps on the carpet as he worked around the room. From the thuds, he never seemed to linger in any one place for long. The drawers opened with the creaking only old wood produced.

The sound of hurried assembly mingled with a match strike—a subtle smell of fire entered the air. Natalie felt twin to the match flame as it found the wick. Light vanilla and jasmine scents wafted through the room.

She smiled without opening her eyes. "You have candles? I assume you weren't planning for a power outage."

"I was planning—hoping—for this." His footsteps came closer, closer still until his breath caressed her face. He took her hand. "You can open them."

The world, blurry at first, was ablaze.

One blink. Two.

Then her eyes adjusted, revealing a fairyscape of winking, twinkling candles scattered all around the room, seeming to occupy every available surface.

Pink and white rose petals decorated the floor,

around the bed. Decadent chocolates swirled in elaborate designs on a silver plate, and imported sparking water glimmered in the light.

She was touched that he'd planned this—and curious. "You were mighty certain we would be back here."

"I wanted to be prepared, just in case, since options for pampering you have been limited." He held her face in both palms. "And trust me, lady, I very much want to shower you in meals and travel and gifts and a million other ideas, if you would just let me."

The thought of that made her head swirl with the complications and problems that would arise from juggling that lifestyle with her children. Sure, people with kids lived fast-track lives, but she didn't. And Colby also thrived on routine. Each thought made her more tense. She had to stop thinking about tomorrow if she expected to enjoy tonight.

She cupped his mouth. "Sweet, but not necessary. I'm not here because of what you can buy me. It's not about money." She waved a hand around the room. "All of this is thoughtful. That's what makes it special. That's what makes *you* special."

"I take that to mean you'll get naked with me." A crooked smile spread across his face. He breathed the words onto her skin, plucking the already-loose dress.

How ironic that he was a cyberguru and after her confidential chat with Margie, the internet had proven to be a helpful source of info on how to relax.

And the best part? The more she slept with Max, the more her body would accommodate him, the more pleasure she would find—and being with him had already been mighty damn satisfying.

Now that she'd done her research, she felt freer, ready.

"I consider it a race to see who can get their clothes off first." She couldn't work fast enough to liberate herself from her sundress, nerves pushing her onward. Delighted by his gesture. By the candles. She'd raced into intimacy headlong in a selfish need to indulge herself after the year of hardship and grief. But now her focus was on Max and the step they were going to take... together. Natalie unzipped her dress as he flung his T-shirt to the far corner of the room, revealing that muscled chest. Damn. Desire pulsed in this momentary pause of appreciation.

"I'm a competitive man. Very competitive." A deep, throaty laugh. With ease, he kicked aside his shorts and boxers, the discarded clothes joining his exiled T-shirt.

She pulled in a breath scented with his aftershave and vanilla candles, savory and sweet. Her heart raced at the sight of him. Endlessly masculine. Impressively confident.

He made her feel more sure of herself, too. His ease with himself. His generous touch. All the ways he was comfortable in his own skin helped her to relax. She knew from her research that was the key to being with him. To resolving the sensual issue that had worried her the first time.

"Lucky me." She arched against him, wiggling out of the gold-toned panties until the two of them were flesh to flesh. Her breasts took in the sweet, gentle abrasion of his chest hair, which teased her nipples to tight, sensitive peaks.

His calloused hands slid down her back to her bottom and lifted her against him.

She viewed that as the very best kind of invitation to wrap her legs around his waist.

"Sweet," he growled against her mouth.

She melted against him, breathing into the moment, determined to wrest every amount of pleasure from this night. And yes, giving pleasure had its own rewards, better than any chocolate treat.

Natalie dug her heels into his back as he walked them toward the bed, her loose hair swaying along her spine.

"Hurry," she urged against his mouth. "We can have slow with flowers and chocolates, too."

She reached down to snag a condom off the bed-side table.

He growled in approval and backed her against the door, freeing one of his hands as she clamped tighter with her legs. She couldn't resist watching as he rolled the sheath down the turgid length. A shiver of antici-pation—and yes, even a hint of apprehension—rippled through her. She breathed, willing the tensed muscles to ease. Max pressed his hand to the door, his legs braced, his erection nudging against the moist core of her.

Breathing, sighing, her head back against the panel, she welcomed him into her body, gravity gently working its magic as he lowered her, filling her. She hooked her ankles and pressed him the rest of the way home. And oh, yes, this was good, so much better than good. Each slickened thrust sent shimmers of sensation through her starved senses.

Tremors began quaking soon, all too soon. Even knowing she would have him again tonight, she wanted to draw out this wild moment as long as possible. It seemed that the past couple of days had been a pro-tracted foreplay leading to this. He eased away and stared deeply into her eyes with an intensity that built her need to a taut point that just...couldn't...be...denied.

Finally—thank goodness, finally—he kissed her,

fully, thoroughly, and thrust into her with a thick abandon that sent her over the edge without warning.

She bit her lip to hold back a cry of bliss with each
wave cresting through her. Her heels dug into his butt
as she angled harder into the sensation. His breathing was ragged, urgent. Max moved faster, launching
aftershocks. His shout of completion spurred a final
wash of pleasure through her. Goose bumps prickled
along her flesh, sparks shimmering inside, as well.
His forehead fell to rest on the door, his cheek against
her hair.

Replete, her body went limp. She kept her arms
locked around his neck as they stood together silently
for more heartbeats than she could count.

Then he released her and her feet slid to the floor.
She started to lose her balance, her body still too sated
to hold her.

Smiling, Max scooped her into his arms as he had
before. "I have you. Relax."

Her body humming with approval, she kissed his
chest just over his pounding heart. Later, they could
talk.

As he lowered her to the petal-strewn bed, her senses
lit at his thoughtfulness. The petals were satiny, but
scented. He'd done such a lovely thing in preparing
without assuming. She was taking one day at a time—
and today was amazing and filled with passionate hope
that for the moment edged out her concerns about protecting her children, her independence, her heart.

He smoothed stray locks back from her face, his
eyes flaming over her. "You're so beautiful. Touching
you turns me inside out. Hell, just the feel of your silky
hair gliding through my fingers makes my teeth ache
from wanting you."

Clearing her throat, she stretched out beside him, their legs tangled. "You don't have to speak and convince me." Her hands fell to rest on his broad shoulders, then she looped her arms around his neck. "I'm here and, yes, I can't deny we've both had chemistry from the moment we first met. I don't understand the why of it all. It just is."

"Some things don't need to be analyzed." His thick thigh nudged higher between her legs, a delicious weight and pressure.

"That's ironic coming from a techie." She chuckled lightly against his kiss.

He combed his fingers through her hair again, light crackles of static snapping through the air. "Business, computers, codes are the last things I'm thinking about when I'm with you."

"Hmm." She savored the feel of his bare skin against her, his hard, muscled body pressing her into the mattress.

"You know what I want now?" She linked hands with him.

His body tensed, his fiery eyes full of determination. "Name it. I'll make it happen."

She lifted his hand and kissed the back of it, then nipped his thumb. "I want that chocolate over there—and more of you."

Warm water streamed down Max's face, steam filling the shower stall, and he gave a prayer of thanks for the tankless water heater that made it possible to stay in this shower with Natalie even longer still. He'd come a long way from the kid who'd waited in line for his turn in the bathroom, often behind a half-dozen other people. Yeah, he liked hot water. A lot.

And he liked being under that spray with Natalie even more.

It had been a natural progression, from bed to shower. All in the effort of cleaning up.

Sex had been great before. But after tonight...

A line in the sand had been drawn—their rhythms and chemistry syncing.

Heart pounding, he recalled when they'd eased into the stall in his private bathroom. He'd guided her in with a strong, stable arm, made sure she didn't slip on the beige tile as her smile—demure, once upon a time— turned feral with that arching eyebrow. She'd immersed herself in the water, enjoying every moment.

No one had ever been sexier. He was convinced of that.

Max wanted this borrowed time to last longer. Especially when she kissed him thoroughly like that.

As she leaned into him in the shower, Max took in a deep breath, the sensation of steam filling his lungs. Chest expanding, he wrapped his arms around her, spun her around to meet his still hungry stare. She seemed just as eager, just as awake as he was. Thick spirals of red hair settled on her back once she stopped spinning. He felt the wild abandon in her green-eyed gaze and it damn near singed his hair.

He kissed her deeply, his tongue grazing hers. Her kiss was literally sweet—chocolate still present in her breath.

They'd moved to another level, one where he suspected a two-week affair wasn't going to be long enough. Which presented a problem. He had to go home, back to work, while her home and work were clearly here.

Sure, he could return to Royal, Texas, every now

and again, but that wasn't sustainable. And she wasn't a booty call. So he needed to start exploring other ways they could see each other. And if she wasn't comfortable with those options outside her newly adopted hometown?

He refused to entertain the notion of defeat. He hadn't built a multimillion-dollar corporation from pure sweat and grit by thinking negatively or admitting defeat easily.

He stroked back her wet hair. "Now, let's figure out where you want to go for our next date. New Orleans? Miami? Or maybe you'd like to go west? Las Vegas? Chicago?"

When she was quiet for a long moment, he acknowledged maybe those spots weren't the most kid-friendly. He tried to think of what would appeal to a young mother and came up with a new angle. "An RV trip to take in some national parks? I hear Yellowstone is something to see."

"Why so far-flung?" she asked him at last. "There are plenty of local places we could go." Switching spots with him, she leaned against the tile, arms crossed over her chest.

He regretted putting her on the defensive even more than he mourned losing the view of her beautiful breasts. Gently, he untwined her arms and stepped back into them. "I have a personal jet. Anywhere is local. Would you like to go overseas? We can do that as well with an extra day's notice if you need to arrange things with the kids. Surely you take an occasional day off from work."

A dismissive smile appeared on her lips. "You're overwhelming me. I'm a simple, small-town girl."

He lowered his lips to her face. Kissed her cheek,

nose, forehead. In a too quiet voice, he made his plea. "And you also moved around the country. I grew up simply, too. If you don't want to do a tourist kind of date, we could go to Seattle...my home."

The water pattered on the stall floor. Otherwise, their steam-filled world stayed silent for more than a few heartbeats.

Finally, she swiped shower spray from her eyes and said, "You're moving things along at light speed when I think we've already moved mighty fast."

"Okay, I'll concede this is a quick step forward, but, Natalie, you have to know I can't stay here indefinitely. I have a business to run back in Seattle. But I'm not ready to call our time together just a fling."

Natalie was worth so much more than such a flippant description. "What if that's all I can give you?"

Her words slapped over him in an icy wave as if the hot-water tank had just run out. He forced himself to stop and think, to study her face rather than just react. As he looked deeper into her eyes, he saw the contradiction to her words.

He saw vulnerability.

Protectiveness pumped through his veins. He was right in pursuing her. He just needed to persuade her. "Trust me on this, Natalie. We can have more than a couple of nights and one dinner out."

Her throat moved in a long swallow. "When I wake up each morning, it's all I can do to think through twenty-four hours. And that's because dough has to rise for the next day's breakfast. I don't have the energy to think longer than that. Maybe it's because hope saps my reserves. Perhaps that makes me a coward—"

"You're one of the strongest people I've met, and I

have come across some of the toughest of the tough in the business world."

"Thank you. Regardless, though, I can't promise you anything more than one day at a time."

He needed to retreat for the moment, and he knew it. He wouldn't push his luck so hard that it cost him this woman. He straightened, finding that familiar devil-may-care smile that had gotten him this far. "Twenty-four hours at a time? I can live with that."

"Seriously?"

"Yes, give me twenty-four hours to convince you we can enjoy twenty-four more on our own, away from here, just the two of us." He sealed his mouth to hers, water sheeting down his back, trickling over them as he backed her against the tile wall. "Mmm..." He moaned against her mouth, then said hoarsely, "Can you arrange an overnight sitter? Or would you like to take the kids? I can hire a nanny."

She leaned her head back against the tile, water clinging to her eyelashes as she blinked them open, full of passion. "I think it's best the kids stay in familiar settings for now. You're new to their world. For that matter, you're new to my world. I don't usually—"

He pressed a finger to her lips. "You don't need to explain anything. I understand. Now, where do you want to go?"

She kissed his fingertips, staring at him. "Vegas sounds fun."

"Vegas it is."

A shift in her eyes matched the twitch in her lips. "But I was actually thinking perhaps Seattle. If it's not an encroachment on your space, I would like to see your home."

Not at all what he had anticipated. But a home-turf

advantage? He could handle that. "I would like to show you my home and my offices."

"What about the investigation here?"

"Actually, I've hit such a brick wall on that, I'm thinking fresh eyes would help. I had already been considering consulting with my CTO—chief technology officer—Will Brady. This would be the perfect time for him to scope out the town and data collected with objective eyes, without me here to skew his impressions. Then when you and I finish our date trip, Will and I can put our heads together."

"You are quite the multitasker." Her words barely registered as she pressed her mouth to his with another kiss.

He'd won the battle here, if not the war. A victory. For now, he could accept that much.

But for how long?

Tall snowcapped peaks stood as sentinels, providing a backdrop for Seattle that seemed, to Natalie's eyes, magical. The jutting mountains and deep green pines bit into the clear blue sky. An impossible blue rendered crisper from the cool weather in the Pacific Northwest. She had no doubt she would experience Seattle's infamous gray skies, but for now, in the moment of her arrival, the sky stretched before her. Endless possibilities.

Or perhaps that more accurately described her feelings about this trip.

She hoped her time here could help reassure her of ways she and Max could be together, ways they could blend their two very different lifestyles.

She vacillated between hopelessness and total optimism and back again, over and over. Perhaps because she'd had too much time to think while traveling on her own. Max had flown out early on a chartered jet because of a work emergency while Natalie had settled her children, and tried hard not to chicken out over flying on his private jet.

At least no one had outright questioned her. The knowledge in their eyes was clear, though. Gossip spread like wildfire in a small town. Everyone in Royal had known she was dating Max, so she gave up trying to keep their relationship quiet.

Both the town and her B and B were abuzz with her news. Even her friend Brandee had called the trip "serious."

Settling deeper into the limo's leather seat, she bristled at the word *serious*, turning the weight of the word over in her mind. Natalie's heart was still heavy from the loss of her husband and the marriage that had started to fray. Her children at least seemed to accept that Max was a "friend."

Her eyes flicked from the mountains to the buildings, noting the way bookstores, tech companies, music venues and coffee shops pressed into each other. It was a spread of literary and tech culture merging together.

Undeniably beautiful. A place she could enjoy visiting…but living here? She shook off the thought. She needed to be in the moment and not make decisions quickly either way.

Fluffing her scarf around her neck, she caught a glance of her reflection in the dark window of the limo Max had arranged to be waiting for her when the flight landed. Her skin glowed brighter—the result of some serious pampering at a spa. Much needed, she'd realized, during the massage.

Her dear new friends—Brandee and Emily—absolutely insisted on treating her to a spa day. They said she worked too hard, spent too much energy on everyone else. "Where is that attention to you?" Emily had asked, her brows arched heavenward. When Natalie didn't respond, they had arranged for a sitter and whisked her away to the day spa for relaxation.

And a makeover.

Her friends had recruited fellow TCC member Naomi Price, a stylist with her own local TV show, who'd brought in racks and racks of incredible designer duds. They'd even commandeered Royal's St. Tropez Salon. It had been a fun and magical experience. She would be lying to herself to think otherwise.

Gazing at the shadowed reflection in the window, she realized that her apprehension didn't just stem from being whisked away to Seattle, or having so many people so publicly aware of her dating life. Those were factors, of course.

But the brimming tension in her tummy came from wondering what he'd make of her new haircut—the shorter strands of strawberry that framed her face called more attention to her green doe eyes.

She touched the silky strands that still seemed slightly chilled, despite the warmth of the limousine.

As Natalie surveyed the skyline, she smiled. Bold buildings—as bold as the mountains in the background—seemed to erupt into the sky. Nothing demure or subdued about this space.

It suited him, she thought to herself.

Much like the small B and B suited her and her children. How strange the way people took on the qualities of their geographies.

Natalie inhaled, absently drinking in the way couples huddled to each other in the cold weather. Texas had yet to become this chilly—it was still only late September.

She wondered how her children were doing without her, even though she knew they were fine thanks to constant text updates and photos.

Margie had offered to watch the children while Natalie visited Max. Over these past few months, the dog trainer had become family—a mother she didn't have. A mother she self-selected. There were no words to convey her level of appreciation for that, or for how wonderful she was with both of Natalie's kids, especially with Colby. Margie even offered to stay at the B and B, which would be the least disruptive to Colby's routine. And if anything were to go wrong overnight at the B and B, Margie could attend to that, as well.

Brandee, Emily and Max's good friend Chels had offered to run the B and B in her absence. Her heart squeezed as she realized how lucky she was to have such friends in her life.

Small gestures were all she had ever had to offer. Small, intentional gestures. Natalie left Margie a fresh-baked casserole for breakfast, tons of fruit already sliced and diced and her to-die-for strudel. She'd also made Emily, Brandee and Chels strudel, as well. A small thank-you, but she'd poured her soul into the baking.

As they drew closer to the St. Cloud tower, her heart beat wildly, disrupting her normally steady demeanor. Shiny black glass dressed the spire in a dark elegance. Power seemed to cling to every aspect of the building, which was as mysterious and seductive as its owner.

The limo driver pulled up to the sidewalk, hopped out of the car to let Natalie out. Cold air caressed her cheeks, deepening the newly acquired blush—another result of Brandee and Emily's makeover.

The driver helped her out of the car and handed off

her luggage to the doorman, who ushered her inside, out of the wind.

Max lived in the penthouse. As the elevator rose, her heart sped up, butterflies returning to her stomach. She wondered as they passed the floors that housed his company what he'd be wearing, how he would react to her new look.

The door to the elevator opened with a ding. Her stomach turned with nerves.

There he was. Waiting for her. It looked like he might have been pacing, the way his muscled frame seemed to lurch forward as she met his gaze.

His lips parted ever so slightly. Eyes turning wide, growing with delight. His smile was genuine and deep as he took her hands and looked her up and down. "*Well*, hey."

"Well, hey," she teased back, his obvious pleasure warming her inside and out.

With a quick head shake, Max picked up her bags from the doorman, eyes staying fixed on her as she stepped through the threshold. And the second the door closed, he took her by the hand again and swung her into his arms. His kiss was fast, intense, deep.

Familiar.

They'd crossed into a new realm. A relationship. This was real. Toe curlingly so. She kissed him back with a familiarity that strummed her senses.

His hands skimmed down her spine and up again. "I missed you."

"I saw you this morning."

"Hours ago. Too long." He kissed her nose.

She felt her nerves settling at the rightness of being with him. She winked and then looked past him to a huge two-wall corner window sprawled in front of her, revealing a perfect view of the Space Needle. A small gasp leaped from her lips. "You have to know your home is incredible. The view is…indescribably gorgeous. No wonder you love it here."

"It was the logical place to make my mark. A techie mecca, home to companies like Amazon and Microsoft."

Max shrugged in his flannel button-down shirt. A casual look for a casual answer and a man who she was realizing didn't have a typical billionaire glitz she would have expected.

Her mind skated back to his words about Seattle. So he didn't feel attached to the town?

As quickly as she formed the thought, she tossed it away. This was about taking things twenty-four hours at a time. To think about him calling somewhere else home implied something she wasn't able to consider.

Just being here alone with him at all felt…surreal.

He placed her suitcase and his computer bag on the sleek black leather bench by the door. She immediately discarded her scarf, but elected to keep her jacket on. A chill lingered.

"I thought we could eat here tonight, on the balcony. Unless you would prefer to go out and see the city?"

Even though his private jet had been tricked out with every luxury she could have asked for, she'd been too nervous to eat or nap, which left her famished and drained. "Let's eat in tonight. Tomorrow you can give me a quick tour of the city before we fly home."

At least they would get to return to Royal together.

For how long?

She shushed her thoughts again before they could ruin their time together before it even started.

"Supper here, then."

She wondered if he planned to call in a catered meal or if there was something already here. He seemed so in control and not concerned she figured he must have plans A, B and C.

He strode toward the kitchen. Envy for a space like this tugged at her baker's heart. The counter space alone made her drool. But the top-of-the-line steel appliances were stunning—paired perfectly with the industrial aesthetic of the concrete. A chef's stove—gas with additional burners. A wine refrigerator.

What she could do with a kitchen like this at her bed-and-breakfast!

Max opened the refrigerator, eliciting a hiss from the mingling of air. She leaned on the countertop, the concrete cool against her fingertips. He pulled out a parcel wrapped in butcher's paper. "I had the ingredients delivered for me to cook supper for you." He grinned over his shoulder. "I do enjoy my kitchen, so I gotta confess I'm glad you opted to eat in. I ordered beef, since you appeared to like our dinner out."

"I did. Very much, thank you." She appreciated his thoughtfulness in noticing her preferences. "What would you have done if I'd chosen a restaurant instead?"

"I had my assistant make reservations as a backup at two different places." He opened the paper to reveal two generous portions of filet mignon. "Once I get this rib eye seasoned with porcini mushrooms and a rosemary rub, I need to head down to my office briefly. I hope you don't mind. You can make yourself at home here."

"If you don't mind, I would enjoy seeing where you work. Heaven knows you've seen every inch of my place, even the sewing room. If I won't be disrupting employees?" She had to admit, his world intrigued her. A lot.

"There's a private elevator from here to my office. But since it's Saturday, you won't have to meet a bunch of strangers. Most likely just my partner, Will, if he hasn't already left for Texas."

"I'm glad you'll have some help with your partner in Royal." She shifted her weight from right to left. The allure of the window called to her, and she found herself staring at the backdrop again.

"I will appreciate the fresh perspective. I feel as if I've hit a wall with uncovering who's behind the blackmail cyberattacks. After interviewing damn near everyone in town and scouring through all available internet data on them—including some backdoor searches it's best we don't discuss—I've hit a dead end. If I'm, uh, distracted, and missing something obvious, I need to know and I trust Will." He finished seasoning the meat, the spicy scent of garlic lingering in the air.

"Distracted?" She couldn't resist crinkling her nose at him playfully.

As he washed his hands, he tossed a wicked grin over his shoulder. "C'mon. Let me give you the grand tour of my company. I will warn you, it isn't as cozy as your setup."

"I would enjoy seeing your offices very much. And I totally understand that you're unlikely to have crayons and coloring books all over everywhere." She clasped his hand, electricity sparking between them with every touch.

The squeeze he gave her hand confirmed that he felt that connection, too.

He walked to the fireplace and keyed in a code. A large mirror slid to the side, revealing a private elevator. Definitely a different world than her homey bed-and-breakfast.

The elevator moved smoothly down ten floors from his penthouse condo, the doors sliding open to...not what she expected. She'd thought they would step into a lobby, but this elevator led straight to his office.

He shrugged. "It's a time saver. I'm able to slip into the office after hours and I'm able to step into work other times without people stopping me with a million questions. It's efficient."

She raised a hand. "You don't have to defend your wealth to me. You've made a huge success of your life. You should be proud of yourself."

"I do love high-tech toys." He pulled what appeared to be a small remote from his pocket.

Halogen bulbs winked on, flooding the room in bright white. Like his apartment, the space was sleek, embodying the bold architectural flair of Seattle. But with hints of color, hints of him...

A mixed-media Sherlock Holmes–themed painting depicting *A Study in Scarlet* hung behind his desk. No pictures, though.

She made his way toward his desk to inspect whisper-thin computer screens and touch pads. A neat pile of paper. An abacus. Orderly. So different than the chaos of the sewing room. Natalie heard the door click behind her.

She let out a low whistle, taking a turn about the room as she shrugged out of her sweater. "It suits you. What do you have to get done tonight?"

Natalie watched his eyes follow the descent of her fluffy sweater onto the desk. The temperature hadn't changed, but her body was heating.

"Um, I just wanted to show you the place and get, um—" His throat bobbed, eyes lingering on her curves.

Feminine power flamed inside her and she welcomed

the distraction from all the conflicting thoughts tumbling through her mind, jockeying for dominance. She angled back against his desk, crossing her legs at the ankles and holding his gaze. She tilted her head to the side as he approached.

He drew her in, their first embrace since she had arrived. For a moment—an infinity, it seemed like—they shared each other's gazes, drank in the nuances in each iris.

He angled his face toward hers, and his lips grazed her neck. Small kisses. A deep sigh pressed hot air onto her neck as he said, "Actually, I have a lot to do here in my office tonight."

Ten

Max had intended the trip to his office to be a quick stop to pick up work and then return to his penthouse to romance her with dinner on his balcony. Followed by an evening of lovemaking.

Apparently, they were mixing the order of his plans.

Leaving little time for conversation or regrets, Max flattened her back against the door. He kissed her, hard, fast, fully. Reasonable thoughts fell away as fast as her purse thudded to the floor. Heat poured from her lips, pulsing through his veins into a throbbing need.

Now that she'd made it clear she wanted him, he couldn't resist. Finally, he had her here, on his turf, in his domain.

And they were alone. Completely.

She grinned against his mouth. "Here?"

"If that's agreeable to you."

She took a step back, slipping her arms through the sleeves of her dress. "Very agreeable."

As Max watched her dress glide to the floor, he imprinted the memory of her in his brain. Hell, he knew full well, it was seared there for eternity. He would never forget the vision of her perched on the edge of his desk wearing nothing but heels and a do-me smile.

Control was shaky at best. But as he'd learned from her bold approach, her drive matched his. They could do slow later. And later again.

Keeping his eyes on hers, he made fast work of his polo shirt, before kicking off his shoes and slacks. He tugged free his wallet at the last second and placed it beside her on the shiny metal desk, flipping it open and spilling out a couple of condoms.

Damn, he should have put more than two in there. But then there were more in his condo.

He silenced her with his mouth, or maybe it was his hand sliding up a silken thigh, between her legs and finding her damp and ready for him.

Her hand slid down to clasp around him. A shudder rocked through him.

He tucked his arm behind her and swept the desk clear before lowering her back. Her hair spread in a stunning red fan along the stainless steel surface. He knew he would have a damn near-impossible job concentrating on work the next time he sat in that chair.

Natalie lifted a shapely leg and traced a toe down the center of his chest. Manicured red toenails grazed his pecs. His abs. His heart hammered in his ears. She was…incredible.

He tucked his arms under her knees and parted her legs, spreading her, all the while watching her eyes for any hint of protest.

She inched her heels behind him, pushing against his

butt and urging him nearer, nearer still until he slid...
home inside her.

His eyes closed at the warm clamp of her, and then
he angled forward over her, holding his full weight with
his elbows.

She clasped hands with him, linking fingers, squeezing.

And then he couldn't think beyond moving inside her,
holding her hands and restraining his release for as long
as possible. Praying she would find completion soon because he wasn't going there without her and the need to
finish roared through him like engines at full throttle.

He dipped his head to nip along her shoulder. A
groan whispered from her kiss-swollen mouth, filling
the space between them with her breath, faster, fuller,
a flush along her pale skin broadcasting how close she
was to unraveling, until...yes. Her arms flung wide to
grip the edges of the desk. She arched up, her body
tensed, moans of pleasure unrestricted. Yes, she had
found completion.

A good thing, since his orgasm was tougher and
tougher to withhold.

Finally, he allowed himself to plunge deep and hard,
his hoarse growl of completion echoing through the
empty office. His domain. His world.

And his woman.

He couldn't ignore the primal declaration echoing
through his mind, his body, his soul. And in spite of
all the reasons he was wrong for her, he began to think
the time had come to figure out how to make their
worlds merge.

The air didn't chill Natalie as she sat on Max's balcony while he leaned against the rail, thumbing through

work text messages. Despite the colder Seattle weather, she felt comfortable, seemingly heated from within. The passionate night had left her ablaze.

Though Max's portable heater certainly helped re-inforce those thoughts.

The Seattle skyline was flecked and twinkled not with stars, but soft lights of buildings, a living constel-lation. The sounds of traffic echoed from far below, a distant beat that felt dreamlike. This whole night felt like the unreality of the border between sleep and con-sciousness, that temporality of potential and magic.

She sat on a plush lounge chair close to the orange glow of the heater, belly full from a five-star-worthy dinner.

That Max had cooked himself.

He was every bit the chef he'd claimed, his rib eye as fine as anything from a Texas steak house, and the kale salad and Asiago macaroni had both been delectable. And the chef had been every bit as enticing as the food. She'd enjoyed watching him deftly move around the kitchen in simple gym shorts and a T-shirt with a hand towel draped around his neck as he prepared their meal.

Most of all, she enjoyed the new ease that had devel-oped between them. He was still his charming self, but in a more relaxed way with less of an aggressive push.

Although she couldn't deny that the speed of their developing relationship left her head spinning.

A slight wind rustled her loose hair. Strands stuck to her cheek. She pushed them aside and picked up her dessert bowl. The gray dish felt heavy and cold in her hand, a chill finally permeating the heat inside her. She scooted closer to the heater. Wearing Max's shirt might not have been the warmest choice, but she'd indulged, enjoying the sense of being closer to him. Savoring the scent of him clinging to the fabric.

Hunger for him stirred in her anew, and she spooned in the vanilla bean ice cream smothered in berries, feeding at least one appetite. She couldn't help being touched at how he remembered her love of ice cream. The fact that they were learning each other's preferences spoke of a growing intimacy beyond sex.

Was she okay with that? She glanced sidelong at him, watching as the wind stirred his dark hair. He gave her a full-out and genuine smile.

For the first time she really let herself consider the notion of attempting a longer-term relationship.

His phone lit up on the side table with a text, and his smile turned to half wattage as he tapped the cell. "I need to check in with Will soon to make sure he arrived in Royal."

She swallowed, the tart blackberry lingering on her tongue. "Okay, sure. The ice cream and I will keep each other occupied."

Exhaling hard, Max set his own bowl down. Sadness touched his features, carving a line of worry into his brow. "Will's had a rough run of it. He's a new widower and *way* out of his element as a single daddy to an infant girl."

"That's so sad. Single parenting is tough, no question." Flashes of another time, just over a year ago, scrolled through her mind. Of a fateful knock at her door. Somehow the sound of it had held a foreboding before she'd been able to confirm with her eyes what was being delivered. A military notification.

When she'd approached the door, baby on her hip, she'd known answering that knock would forever change her world.

A chilly wind blew across the balcony, almost as cold as the chill inside her from those memories.

She closed her eyes for a moment, willing the painful past away. "How is Will managing his trip to Royal?"

Standing, he looked down at his phone. "He has a full-time nanny for his daughter."

"That's good that he's able to travel with his child." She didn't know how she would have made it through without her children. Those days she'd wanted to curl up under the covers forever, she'd pulled herself from bed each day to take care of Colby and Lexie.

"I didn't mean to say the nanny and baby always travel with him." He scrubbed his hand over his chin. "He's having trouble with grief. I'm sure you understand that."

"Are you saying he's having trouble bonding with his daughter?" Jeremy had had difficulty connecting with Colby. She'd credited that to their son crying so much from colic. Then over time, it had become clear there was more than colic.

Another pang shot through her heart.

Max turned the cell phone over and over in his hand. "Will is a good friend, a good person. He won't abandon his child. Parenting is—and should be—a lifelong commitment." He held up his phone. "I need to check in with him. It won't take long."

She waved her spoon. "Don't rush on my account. I have plenty here to keep me occupied."

Natalie turned her attention back to the night skyline as she heard the sliding glass door rumble open, matching Max's baritone voice as he spoke into the phone. His voice faded, leaving her once again to the quiet of Seattle's night viewed from a penthouse height.

Taking in the magnificence of the Space Needle,

she turned his words over in her head about parenting. She appreciated that he understood that responsibility. Which, of course, he did, given his childhood that had left him abandoned by both his father and his mother.

But parenting as just a responsibility?

There was more. Another element. Love.

It was so important for children to feel their parents' love. Jeremy had tried with Colby, but he'd clearly felt a closer bond to Lexie and it had broken Natalie's heart to see the disparity.

She couldn't help noticing how Max tried equally with both of her children. He didn't give himself credit, but she could see his ease with both children, feel that he genuinely cared about people without reservations or judgment.

He was a good man.

A good man who lived in Seattle in a concrete palace. The balcony had an idyllic view, but the small space confined by rails clearly wasn't designed with children in mind. But there was so much space beyond here, out there in Seattle. Could she live here? Could he move his business to Texas?

Could he open his heart to her children?

Her stomach knotted and the spoon rattled back into her bowl. Had he imagined Max's connection to her children? Because when he was with her family, she couldn't deny that it felt right. Good. She owed it to herself—and her children—to at least give this relationship a serious chance. She could always invite him back to Cimarron Rose one last time just to see where it led...

What the hell was she thinking letting her thoughts travel those kinds of paths? Visiting Max was about having a fling. Wasn't it?

She'd just started to find her way in the world again,

learning how to build a good life for her children on her own. After the heartbreak of her marriage, did she have the courage to try for more again?

Back in Royal less than a week later, Max juggled two juice boxes in one hand while he held open Natalie's refrigerator, looking for the fresh apple turnovers that Natalie had left in the fridge. A surreal wave washed over him.

She trusted him. Implicitly. After being hesitant to allow him to be around her children, Natalie had left them in his care while she went to Brandee Lawless's house for a fitting. He'd helped load the car full of lacy material, measuring tapes and a sketchbook.

He smiled inwardly, recalling the way her nose had crinkled as she showed him the toy cabinet and location of all the supplies he would need for his childcare adventure. She'd kissed him deeply, been so appreciative of his help.

And he would not let her down. Picking up the apple turnover platter with his other hand, he turned to face Lexie and Colby.

Lexie twirled and twirled and twirled in her little pink dress.

"Mr. Max! Mr. Max! Look." She leaped, almost like a ballerina.

"That's perfect, kiddo. What do you say we eat some apple turnovers in the living room? Maybe watch some TV?" He smiled at her. So much energy out of one little body. He had to give Natalie even more credit than ever before. Taking care of two little kids was tougher, more exhausting, than any day he'd put in at the office. And she managed this while running a business.

He couldn't even claim that distraction, since the

B and B was empty for the morning, a slew of new guests due later in the day, the reason Natalie had opted to do the fitting now. She'd figured watching the kids would be easier.

Ha.

"Yeah, TV, TV, TV," Lexie squealed, clapping her hands as she bolted off to the living room in a blur of pink.

Colby shifted on his feet, looked at him. "Can we watch *Fishtales*?"

The question had caught him off guard, the way the boy was warming to him rather than just answering questions. "Of course we can, Colby."

"Cool." A rare smile tugged at his little mouth. Miss Molly nuzzled her charge's hand. Colby patted the side of his leg. "Come, Miss Molly. Let's go."

The trio walked to the living room. Lexie and Colby sat on the couch and sank into the cushioning. Max placed the plate of turnovers in front of them. Miss Molly, who had lain at Colby's feet, eyed the plate. Praying for crumbs probably.

Max thumbed the television remote, pulled up *Fishtales* and hit Play. He settled into the armchair, content. They could blend their worlds, bring them together. Natalie had spent time with him in Seattle, and now here he was back in Texas, figuring out the domestic scene.

Things could actually be this good. He swiped one of the apple turnovers, enjoying the spice of the cinnamon and the fresh apples. Calm. Everything was calm.

Until his phone vibrated three times in a row. Retrieving it from his pocket, he saw he'd just missed a call from Will.

A break in the case? Looking back at Natalie's children, he watched as they stared intensely, enthralled by a cartoon movie.

He would only be gone a few moments. He quietly excused himself, careful not to disturb their TV time.

Max made his way into the hall and pressed the call-back option on his phone. The phone rang once before Will's gruff voice answered.

"Hey, I just wanted to let you know we've gotten a significant amount of data from the algorithm you designed. I think that we might be onto something," Max's friend said by way of answering. Will was no-nonsense, always down to business.

Though Max could barely hear his friend over Miss Molly's whining. The dog came, nuzzled his hand. Whined again. Ran to the door and barked, distracting him from what Will was saying.

"I'm sorry, Will. Could you hold on a second?" Max asked, looking at the dog. Then back to the living room.

And only seeing Lexie.

He tamped down worry that threatened his focus and started walking through the downstairs, checking the bathrooms while his friend repeated whatever he'd said before. But Max couldn't think about the conversation or the case. Each step through the Cimarron Rose only hammered home that he didn't know where Colby had gone and there were no guests around who might have seen him or could help him look.

Miss Molly's scratching grew more frantic, and was now partnered with barking. Max jogged back to the kitchen and looked out the windows. Still no sign of Colby.

To hell with calm.

Panic surged through him. "Will, I have to call you

back." He hung up, moving to the door where Miss Molly scratched.

Damn. He'd turned his back for a minute. Maybe two.

But it had been enough time for Colby to leave, slip out the back door. Maybe if Max had paid attention to Miss Molly's whining sooner...

The thought chilled him. Grabbing Lexie by her hand, he ushered her outside, his heart pounding as they walked out the back door. His trained sleuth eyes scanned the horizon for any sign of the boy.

All the while, fear knotted in his chest. This was absolute failure. Never had he sunk so low, lost so much.

This wasn't a failed case. He couldn't locate Natalie's child. He'd let her down more than he could articulate. He'd made a mistake in thinking he could step into this family and be a positive influence. He'd hurt the woman he cared about in the worst possible way.

"Colby. Colby," he shouted, voice bellowing and echoing in the cool September air.

His heart hammered harder, faster. He called for Colby again and again, searching around the yard, in the bushes. The street was clear, but, God, he couldn't even stomach the thought of Colby out on a busy road.

"Colby," he shouted again.

Still, nothing. Not a sound came back. Except for the distinct sound of car tires on pavement. Natalie had come home, parking in the back as she usually did. He didn't even want to think about how terrified she would be. Right now he had to focus on the possibility that Colby would come out of hiding for his mother.

Hitching Lexie up to hold and be sure he didn't lose this one, too, he started toward Natalie. Saw her process the scene, the fear on her face registering as she exited the car. She knew, even before he opened his mouth.

Leaving the car door open behind her, Natalie ran toward the next-door neighbors. "The Albertsons. He likes their cat."

Max sprinted to catch up, a few steps behind her. He'd scanned the neighboring yards and hadn't seen the boy...but had he looked where a cat might be?

His gaze tracked up and...

"There," Max said, pointing at the Albertsons' tree, where Colby lingered. He was holding a branch, his feet braced against the trunk, ready to climb. Natalie rushed to her son and pulled him down. She hugged Colby hard, her fear for him clearly having overcome her normal restraint in giving the boy his space.

Miss Molly bounded over and nudged the mother and son. To comfort Colby? Or for Natalie? Either way, thank God, Colby had been found.

Max gripped the picket fence, more than a little unsteady. Relief washed through him.

Miss Molly pushed between Natalie and Colby. As Natalie rocked back on her heels, the sun glinted along a tear streaking down her face. That lone droplet clinging to her chin gutted Max.

Her devastated face said it all. She'd trusted him with her children and he'd failed. Failed her and failed the children.

"God, Natalie," he said hoarsely, setting Lexie back on the ground. "I'm sorry. So sorry."

Sorry for more than the moment. Sorry he couldn't be the man this family needed.

Eleven

As the door to Lexie's room clicked shut, Natalie let loose a breath she hadn't realized she'd held. The air expelled from her lungs, her chest deflating, taking with it some of the tension.

She ran a hand through her hair, letting the silken strands slip between her fingers, gaze shifting from Lexie's door to Colby's.

Thank God he was safe.

He'd slipped away before. A few times. Each time brought more panic to her lungs, to her limbs. She'd have to watch him more carefully—and warn newcomers about his tendency to sneak off.

Panic had held her chest in a tight knot in those few moments they searched for him. Now she crept to the door, just to make sure one last time that he was there.

Cracking the door open, she peered inside. She was comforted by Miss Molly's perked ears at the sound of her intrusion, and by the sight of Colby's sleeping body.

Satisfaction. Relief. Both those sensations filled her until her breath returned to a normal cadence.

As she turned the corner into the kitchen, her heart sank when another scene of departure greeted her, leaching the warmth from her fingertips. Deep down, she'd known this was inevitable, but still, she'd dared hope. And that hurt like hell.

Max sat at the kitchen table. Lines of anguish and, yes, defeat were carved in his face. His normally easy smile was replaced with a thin hard line. His eyes were downcast, seeming to examine the two leather bags off to the left of his feet.

He met her gaze, noticing her presence. Or maybe he had registered her sharp intake of breath.

While, yes, defeat colored his features, so did a kind of somber resolve. "I'm going to Chelsea's. I've already packed my computer gear. I think it's best."

Natalie blinked. Once. Twice. Tried to discern if this was indeed her reality. "That's it? After chasing me like crazy you're just leaving? I'm not a challenge anymore?"

His broad shoulders braced, his eyes pained but his jaw resolute. "It's not that at all. I'm not right for you, Natalie. I never was. I should have been honest with myself. I'm just not wired for being a part of a family lifestyle and routine."

Natalie couldn't speak, her throat was too clogged with emotion. She could only watch him scan the kitchen, his gaze pausing on Colby's fish drawings that hung haphazardly on the fridge. Total quiet descended, pressing down on the room.

On her.

Finally, he looked back at her, his eyes full of guilt on top of that pain. "Look at what happened today with

Colby getting lost. Who knows how long he could have been out if Miss Molly hadn't alerted me?"

The self-recrimination in his voice tugged her forward a step. She reached to him, her hand shaking, her nerves still rattled. "I should have told you he's an escape artist. I shouldn't have expected you to be a mind reader."

"Don't make excuses for me." He ignored her extended hand. "God knows, I can't make an excuse for myself. I'm sorry, Natalie, so damn sorry." He shook his head, seeming so distant now. His gaze turned inward, examining something she couldn't see. "You deserve better and I'm going to step out of the way so you can have it."

His words hurt, more than she would have expected, given how often she'd thought about how wrong they were for each other. Still, she'd dared to hope—he'd insisted she should. He'd made her live for more than the day. He'd renewed hope and confidence in her.

She was worth more than what he was giving her right now. He'd wanted her to take a risk, and now that she had done so, he was bailing.

Well, damn it, she wasn't letting him go that easily. "That sounds like a cop-out excuse to me. I told you I don't blame you. No one expects you to be an instant child expert in a few days. You're selling yourself short and just giving up. Giving up on us, giving up on a chance at the family you were robbed of in your early years." As she said the words, she found herself voicing the possibility in her heart, too. Yes, she'd dared to hope maybe they could work this out into a future that promised more. "There's a real possibility you could have that if you weren't so willing to walk away."

His jaw worked as he held her gaze for so long she

thought he might actually have heard her. She could see the war in his eyes, see that he was moved. Then he tore his gaze from hers and looked away, shaking his head. "You've been hurt too much, Natalie. And your kids deserve better. I'm a techie, a man of facts and probabilities, so I can calculate odds. All that training tells me, in no uncertain terms, I'm just not worth the risk."

Without meeting her gaze, he picked up his bags and walked out of her life.

Tension had been her constant companion since Max left four days ago. Her decision to call him out on running away still was the right one. Of that she felt certain.

Living with her parents' disappointment in her had finally given her the strength to see that she was a good parent. That she could raise her kids on her own and do a damn good job of it. She wouldn't settle for a man in her life who wasn't ready to shoulder the normal fears that came with parenting. But knowing she'd made the right call didn't do a damn thing to soothe the ache of missing Max.

Four days. It seemed like such a short amount of time.

And she missed him a helluva lot. Felt that longing in her chest, in the way her eyes absently, yet actively searched the parking lot for his rented SUV.

Even now, with Margie, she still found herself occasionally diverting her eyes from the yard. To the room where he'd spent so much time. To that other life she had glimpsed.

"I miss seeing Max around here." Margie tossed the tennis ball to Lexie, who giggled as she half caught, then dropped it. The golden autumn sun provided just enough warmth to warrant a light jacket, even beneath the shade of the tree.

Miss Molly barked in excitement as Lexie scooped up the ball and tossed it with a strong pitch born of much practice at the game.

"Max and I are no longer an item. It was...a risk. That happens. Not every relationship turns into forever. Our lives are in different places," Natalie said in a cool voice that made her seem much more collected than she felt. Miss Molly dropped the ball at Lexie's pink sneakers.

Margie looked at her sidelong, that knowing expression in her keen eyes. "Your boyfriend has a private airplane. You're never far out of reach."

Boyfriend. What a surreal word. It sounded like a word of days gone by, a time of innocence before so much pain and loss. "Whatever he was, it's over."

Colby darted in front of them, the golden retriever close at his heels, tail wagging in delight. Her heart pulsed at the sight of her son's smile. Lexie threw the ball back to Margie, catching the pup's attention.

"Oh, sweetie, I know you too well. We're your family now. That's how this town works, making family connections out of strong friendships." Margie took a turn at the game, lobbing the ball farther to give the dog more of a workout. "I guess that's what makes this hacker's attacks hurt all the more, since it means someone in our 'family' betrayed us. We all have secrets, so we're all vulnerable."

A gust of wind rustled the yellow and red leaves that peppered the still-green yard. The scent of pinecones and the distant scent of a bonfire carried on the wind. This small town offered her a haven. "Margie, I'm finding it tough to believe you have any dark secrets."

A deep laugh shook the older woman's shoulders. She tugged on the sleeve of her red-and-black-plaid shirt, eyes wide and kind. "Oh, honey, there are some, how shall we say it, boudoir photos I had made for my husband's birthday about twenty years ago. I never could find the negatives when I went through his belongings after he passed away."

"Oh, my." Natalie couldn't help grinning—and she also couldn't help marveling at the way Margie managed to smile over memories of her dead husband, to even joke over going through his things.

"Exactly." Margie let out a low, exaggerated sigh. "Every time I see a pink boa, I have twinges of fear of those pictures popping up."

"Pink boa?" Natalie asked, feeling more attached to Margie for her boldness now. A kinship, something like family. The family one chooses.

"And bubble-bath pictures." Her eyes twinkled for a moment. "My Terence sure did love that gift, though."

"Sounds like you had a wonderful marriage." Her heart squeezed at being denied that dream not once, but twice.

Margie's gaze went to the street, to a passing yellow truck. The sputtering sound of the engine filled the conversation for a few heartbeats. In a quiet voice, she nodded, blinking back tears. "We did."

"You were lucky." Was it so wrong to want a happily-ever-after for herself? A family life for her children?

Natalie's eyes flicked to the scene in front of her. Happy dog, happy children. This small town that provided them shelter. And yet...she wanted more.

"Some of it was luck. A lot of it was hard work."

Natalie bristled, ruffled to think that Margie was suggesting she wasn't trying enough now.

"Hard work isn't always enough." She and Jeremy had struggled. She liked to think they would have made things work, but she would never know for sure.

"I realize that, honey. But without the work, even luck won't pull you through. By giving it your one hundred percent, you do have the reassurance of knowing you did everything possible. And that's all we can ever control in life—what we do." She patted Natalie's cheek. "Be at peace with yourself about Jeremy, dearie. You deserve it."

How had Margie read her mind so clearly? The woman sure hadn't been joking about forging a family bond out of friendships. But then hadn't Max said the same about the foster father who taught him how to cook? That had been a family for Max.

A family Max had lost.

And in that thought, realization sank in. Max did know how to be a part of a family. And just as she had lost, so had he. That big bold man really was afraid of being hurt again.

Like she'd been doing, he was protecting his heart. Because yes, she loved him and she suspected he was falling in love with her.

Margie's words reverberated in her mind, about the only way to escape regrets was to give her all. She'd let Max walk out that door. She'd let the man she loved walk away.

And the only way she could be at peace with how her future played out was to know she hadn't left anything unsaid. She was strong enough to stand up for herself, for her children, for Max.

And for a chance at the future they deserved to have. Together.

A plan formed in her head, a way to start at least.

Parenting an autistic child had taught her she couldn't wait for problems to work themselves out. She had to be involved in positive change. To make the world a better place for her child. She needed to act. Maybe now she needed to take action for herself.

"Margie, did you mean what you said about us being family?"

"Of course, dear." Margie squeezed her hand. "What do you need?"

"Can you take the kids for the evening?" She reached into her pocket for her cell phone. "Given Colby's tendency to wander off, I need to upgrade my security system. And I believe St. Cloud Security Solutions has just the right person to install the best of the best."

In spite of his resolution to do right by Natalie and keep his distance, here he was again, at the Cimarron Rose.

Max thumbed the strap of the leather bag that he'd slung over his shoulder, taking comfort in the security gear inside. Most of his work focused on cybersecurity and grounds security for large corporations. But keeping Natalie and her kids safe? His most important job.

He'd leaped at her request that gave him a reason to be right where he'd been longing to be every second since he'd left. Even working like hell with Will and with Chels's brother, Daniel, hadn't provided the distraction he sought. Will and Daniel had all but thrown him out when the call came for a basic security-system install at Natalie's.

He approached the white picket-fence gate, drawing in a deep breath. He looked at the constellations in the night sky, taking reassurance from their twinkling as he did when he'd been on the street.

The night sky had always called to him, giving him constancy in a turbulent life.

He knew this wasn't his wisest move ever coming here. But when Chelsea told him Natalie needed a security system to keep Colby safe? There'd been no way Max could turn his back, or even send over Will. He would make Natalie's house as safe as it could be. Make her kids safe.

The past days without Natalie had been hell. The hole in his life a gaping wound. He still wasn't sure what to do—an anomaly for a man like him—but he also knew he couldn't keep hiding out at Chelsea's while he looked for the hacker.

He made a move to go to the door, then noticed the spotlight on in the backyard.

An awareness coiled in his stomach. Natalie was in the backyard. Probably on that glider with a glass of wine. Just as she'd been his first night.

He adjusted his course, made his way to the backyard. Needing—not just wanting—to see her.

His chest tightened as his eyes found her and took in the familiar sight of Natalie, feeling like it had been months since he'd seen her rather than days. Looking at him without speaking, she tapped the glider back and forth, her silver sandals glinting in the moonlight. Her sapphire-blue dress grazed her ankles, and strawberry curls fell loosely over her shoulders. She held a narrow goblet and rested it lightly on her knee.

A beer waited for him on the tree-stump end table. She'd taken a huge risk to her pride for him. Her giving heart and her confidence were…stunning.

Her calm face called him closer.

He made his way across the lawn, crunching leaves,

and then dropped his computer bag at her feet. "I hear you need a security upgrade."

Not his best opening line.

She gestured to the longneck bottle. "Have a drink and let's talk about what I need."

Had she meant the double entendre?

He took the beer and sat beside her. "I got your message from Chelsea." He glanced at her. "What would you have done if I'd sent Will?"

She smiled. "You didn't."

"I have trouble saying no to you." He took a risk and tucked a lock of her hair over her shoulder. His fingers ached for the familiar softness of her skin. "It's been like that since I first saw you. I want to give you everything. You deserve it, Natalie."

She took his hand in hers, looking at him with those clear green eyes. "That's ironic, since you're taking away the one thing I want most. You."

Hers words pierced right through him. Even more than the wind that whipped and rustled the trees. God, he wanted to cave right now, but he loved her too much—

Loved?

The word stopped him short. *The* word. The one he'd been hiding from since the first second he'd laid eyes on her.

He'd fallen in love with her at first sight. Which was why he was so damn afraid of letting her down. The stakes were the highest ever.

"Natalie—"

She pressed her fingers to his mouth. "I believe you that you would do anything for me. I do." Her fingers grazed down until her palm rested over his pounding heart. "And I don't want to take advantage of that. Instead of us spending so much time seeing how you fit into my life, I think it's time for me to be more open to discussing changes I could make. Seattle was gorgeous. I enjoyed my time there and can imagine spending time there, much more time."

Her willingness to compromise, to give up so much for him, humbled him. Max leaned in, his face so close to hers he could feel her breath on his skin. "And your kids?"

"They have fish and computers and crayons in Seattle. Maybe the kids would enjoy a trip to a cabin as a starter." She held his face, those tender fingers stroking ever so slightly.

God, she totally humbled him with her forgiving, giving, beautiful heart.

"You're really offering this after the way I walked out on you?"

She eased back, resting a hand on his chest again and looking deep into his eyes. Searching. "You're here. That tells me a lot."

A shudder of relief rocked through him, all the way to his core. "I meant it when I said I'm afraid I can't do this, be a parent, be a part of a family. Not after the way I grew up." His life on the streets had left him far from prepared for parenthood. "What if I screw up again? What if I can't give you and the kids enough?"

"Oh, Max—" she smiled, no doubts in her eyes "—we all screw up. That's life. As for your other worry? You're one of the most giving people I've ever met."

"I'm not a role model for your children, not after the things that I've done. I've broken the law more than once in my past." He needed to be sure she didn't see him through rose-colored glasses. He had to be certain *she* was certain, because he didn't think he could scavenge the will to tell her goodbye again.

"What are you doing now? How are you living your life now?" She asked the pointed questions firmly. "You're a good man. I can see that."

"I don't need to survive that way. The choices are easier now."

"I've known plenty of people with money who made less-than-moral choices. Money doesn't determine a person's character. If so, that would make for a sad world." She slipped her hand into his again and held firm. "I've seen the kind of man you are, and everything I've observed is so admirable it takes my breath away."

"You're letting me off the hook too easily." He wanted to believe her, believe it could be this simple. But he was still so damn afraid of hurting her, of letting Natalie and the kids down.

"What do you want for your life, Max?"

"That's too simple a question." He didn't understand how that would fix the problems between them. Didn't see how his wishes did a damn thing to make him the kind of father she needed for her children.

Those cool green eyes seemed to turn to fire. Her gentle features darkened, her brow knitting. "Actually, it isn't. It's a very complex, important question. You're such an ambitious man, such a kingdom builder on a professional level. Why is it so difficult for you to make wishes on a personal level?"

"Because," he admitted the truth through gritted teeth, "losing people hurts more than losing any fortune. It's not worth the risk."

She clasped both his hands in hers and squeezed hard. "Max, I've lost, too. I'm scared, too, believe me." Her exhale was shaky, but her gaze was steady. "But

I'm more afraid of the regrets I'll have if I don't take this risk and ask you. And I'm asking you, what do you want for your life?"

He told himself he wasn't going to do this. Still, he found himself speaking the deepest truth of his heart.

"I want you." The need *was* simple, after all. So damn straightforward and true. "I want to be the kind of man Colby and Lexie deserve to have bringing them up."

"That's an amazing start. What else do you want?"

He cleared his throat and dared say what he wanted most of all. "I want your love."

Her eyes went shiny with unshed tears that glistened with joy. "You have that. Completely." She leaned toward him until their clasped hands touched, heart to heart. "I am absolutely, completely in love with you, Max. St. Cloud."

Relief rushed through him and he kissed her hard, holding, sealing this moment in his mind forever before he whispered against her lips. "And I love you, Natalie Valentine. I swear to you, I am going spend every day of my life proving to you how much I adore you and your children. I'm going to work—"

"Shhh." She kissed him silent. "I know. I believe you. Let's get back to talking about what you want."

Her words surprised him, but the answer was so clear, so right, he wondered why he hadn't dared trust it before. "I want to find a way to be a part of Royal, Texas, and build a cabin home in Washington."

She grinned, surprise coloring her eyes. "A cabin home?"

"A place with a yard and a kick-ass kitchen. A good spot to fish with Colby. A private landing strip on the property so we could fly back and forth with the kids and Miss Molly."

"That sounds like more than a cabin."

He wrapped his arms around her and slid her onto his lap. "When I dream, I dream big, Natalie."

Her arms draped over his shoulders, her fingers toying with his hair. "Big dreams are a good thing."

He grazed his mouth over hers. "And making them come true is even better."

* * * * *

TAKING HOME THE TYCOON
by USA TODAY *bestselling author Catherine Mann*

and

October 2017:
BILLIONAIRE'S BABY BIND
by USA TODAY *bestselling author*
Katherine Garbera

November 2017:
THE TEXAN TAKES A WIFE
by USA TODAY *bestselling author Charlene Sands*

December 2017:
BEST MAN UNDER THE MISTLETOE
by Jules Bennett

If you're on Twitter, tell us what you think
of Harlequin Desire! #harlequindesire

If you enjoyed this book, you'll love
CAN'T HARDLY BREATHE,
the next book in New York Times
bestselling author Gena Showalter's
ORIGINAL HEARTBREAKERS *series.*
Read on for a sneak peek!

MILLS & BOON®
Hardback – September 2017

ROMANCE

The Tycoon's Outrageous Proposal	Miranda Lee
Cipriani's Innocent Captive	Cathy Williams
Claiming His One-Night Baby	Michelle Smart
At the Ruthless Billionaire's Command	Carole Mortimer
Engaged for Her Enemy's Heir	Kate Hewitt
His Drakon Runaway Bride	Tara Pammi
The Throne He Must Take	Chantelle Shaw
The Italian's Virgin Acquisition	Michelle Conder
A Proposal from the Crown Prince	Jessica Gilmore
Sarah and the Secret Sheikh	Michelle Douglas
Conveniently Engaged to the Boss	Ellie Darkins
Her New York Billionaire	Andrea Bolter
The Doctor's Forbidden Temptation	Tina Beckett
From Passion to Pregnancy	Tina Beckett
The Midwife's Longed-For Baby	Caroline Anderson
One Night That Changed Her Life	Emily Forbes
The Prince's Cinderella Bride	Amalie Berlin
Bride for the Single Dad	Jennifer Taylor
A Family for the Billionaire	Dani Wade
Taking Home the Tycoon	Catherine Mann

MILLS & BOON®
Large Print – September 2017

ROMANCE

The Sheikh's Bought Wife	Sharon Kendrick
The Innocent's Shameful Secret	Sara Craven
The Magnate's Tempestuous Marriage	Miranda Lee
The Forced Bride of Alazar	Kate Hewitt
Bound by the Sultan's Baby	Carol Marinelli
Blackmailed Down the Aisle	Louise Fuller
Di Marcello's Secret Son	Rachael Thomas
Conveniently Wed to the Greek	Kandy Shepherd
His Shy Cinderella	Kate Hardy
Falling for the Rebel Princess	Ellie Darkins
Claimed by the Wealthy Magnate	Nina Milne

HISTORICAL

The Secret Marriage Pact	Georgie Lee
A Warriner to Protect Her	Virginia Heath
Claiming His Defiant Miss	Bronwyn Scott
Rumours at Court (Rumors at Court)	Blythe Gifford
The Duke's Unexpected Bride	Lara Temple

MEDICAL

Their Secret Royal Baby	Carol Marinelli
Her Hot Highland Doc	Annie O'Neil
His Pregnant Royal Bride	Amy Ruttan
Baby Surprise for the Doctor Prince	Robin Gianna
Resisting Her Army Doc Rival	Sue MacKay
A Month to Marry the Midwife	Fiona McArthur

0817 GEN STD LP

MILLS & BOON®
Hardback – October 2017

ROMANCE

Claimed for the Leonelli Legacy	Lynne Graham
The Italian's Pregnant Prisoner	Maisey Yates
Buying His Bride of Convenience	Michelle Smart
The Tycoon's Marriage Deal	Melanie Milburne
Undone by the Billionaire Duke	Caitlin Crews
His Majesty's Temporary Bride	Annie West
Bound by the Millionaire's Ring	Dani Collins
The Virgin's Shock Baby	Heidi Rice
Whisked Away by Her Sicilian Boss	Rebecca Winters
The Sheikh's Pregnant Bride	Jessica Gilmore
A Proposal from the Italian Count	Lucy Gordon
Claiming His Secret Royal Heir	Nina Milne
Sleigh Ride with the Single Dad	Alison Roberts
A Firefighter in Her Stocking	Janice Lynn
A Christmas Miracle	Amy Andrews
Reunited with Her Surgeon Prince	Marion Lennox
Falling for Her Fake Fiancé	Sue MacKay
The Family She's Longed For	Lucy Clark
Billionaire Boss, Holiday Baby	Janice Maynard
Billionaire's Baby Bind	Katherine Garbera

MILLS & BOON®
Large Print – October 2017

ROMANCE

Sold for the Greek's Heir — Lynne Graham
The Prince's Captive Virgin — Maisey Yates
The Secret Sanchez Heir — Cathy Williams
The Prince's Nine-Month Scandal — Caitlin Crews
Her Sinful Secret — Jane Porter
The Drakon Baby Bargain — Tara Pammi
Xenakis's Convenient Bride — Dani Collins
Her Pregnancy Bombshell — Liz Fielding
Married for His Secret Heir — Jennifer Faye
Behind the Billionaire's Guarded Heart — Leah Ashton
A Marriage Worth Saving — Therese Beharrie

HISTORICAL

The Debutante's Daring Proposal — Annie Burrows
The Convenient Felstone Marriage — Jenni Fletcher
An Unexpected Countess — Laurie Benson
Claiming His Highland Bride — Terri Brisbin
Marrying the Rebellious Miss — Bronwyn Scott

MEDICAL

Their One Night Baby — Carol Marinelli
Forbidden to the Playboy Surgeon — Fiona Lowe
A Mother to Make a Family — Emily Forbes
The Nurse's Baby Secret — Janice Lynn
The Boss Who Stole Her Heart — Jennifer Taylor
Reunited by Their Pregnancy Surprise — Louisa Heaton

0917 GEN STD LP